Deat
Garden

MW01254941

Hope Callaghan

hopecallaghan.com

*****

Visit my website for new releases and special offers: hopecallaghan.com/newsletter/

A special thank-you to my mother-in-law, Sybil, one of the best Southern cooks on the planet, for sharing her Chicken and Dumplings recipe with me for this book.

i

Contents

Chapter One 1
Chapter Two 50
Chapter Three 59
Chapter Four 86
Chapter Five 95
Chapter Six 107
Chapter Seven 123
Chapter Eight 131
Chapter Nine 156
Chapter Ten 177
Chapter Eleven 189
Chapter Twelve 198
Chapter Thirteen 231
Chapter Fourteen 241
Chapter Fifteen 256
Chapter Sixteen 277
Chapter Seventeen 288
Chapter Eighteen 318
Chapter Nineteen 323
Chapter Twenty 326
Chapter Twenty-One 332
Chapter Twenty-Two 348
Books in This Series 351
Get Free eBooks and More 352
Meet the Author 353
Dot's Delicious Chicken and Dumplings Recipe 354

Chapter One

The first thing Gloria noticed were the police cars surrounding Dot's Kitchen. The second thing she noticed was the police tape. The bright yellow tape with black letters, *POLICE LINE. DO NOT CROSS*.

A cluster of black uniforms with holstered guns plastered to their hips crowded the sidewalk out front and even more were milling about inside. All the parking spots in front of the restaurant were taken. Cop cars, crime scene vans. Some even looked like unmarked police cars.

The closest spot Gloria could find was at the end of Main Street. She pulled Annabelle in next to a Montbay County Crime Scene unit.

Today was Gloria's first chance to make it into the little town of Belhaven after her sister, Liz, led her on a wild goose chase through the

Smoky Mountains. She hoped to meet up with some of the other girls for coffee and find out what her friend, Margaret, and she had missed.

Judging by all the action in front of the restaurant, it looked like they missed a lot.

Gloria's brow furrowed in a deep line as she pushed the car door open. She hoped that Dot and her husband, Ray, were all right.

She locked the door and began the short walk down the sidewalk toward Dot's Restaurant.

There were only two officers standing out on the sidewalk now. They were just on the other side of the police tape, engrossed in conversation. They didn't hear Gloria come up behind them. "... looks like he was poisoned right there at the table."

Her hand flew to her mouth. *Someone in the restaurant had been poisoned*? What if it was someone she knew? The little town of Belhaven was so small, she knew almost everyone that ate there.

A lump lodged in the back of her throat. What if it was Ray?

She tapped one of the officers on the shoulder. "Excuse me..."

The conversation stopped. He turned to face her, his eyebrows raised.

"My friend, Dot. She owns the restaurant. Is she okay?"

The officer nodded. "Last time I checked, the owners were on the back patio."

Gloria let out the breath she'd been holding. At least Dot and Ray were okay. She knew exactly where they were. There was a small, covered patio area with a few picnic tables, just outside the rear entrance. Dot and Ray kept tables out back for the employees to use while on lunch or on break.

She wandered down the alley that ran along the side of the building and made her way to the rear. She rounded the corner and could see her friend, Dorothy "Dot" Jenkins and husband, Ray, seated at one of the tables.

Gloria's heart plummeted when she saw her friend's face buried in her hands, her shoulders shaking uncontrollably. As she got closer, she could hear Ray talking to her in a low voice. "Don't worry, Dot, they will get this all straightened out," he reassured his wife. "We both know you didn't poison anyone."

For a second, Gloria hesitated and then she started to back away, hoping they wouldn't notice her.

She probably would have been able to escape if not for a larger planter which was in her path. She backed straight into it. The metal ornament teetered back and forth in slow motion before it tipped over and hit the cement with a loud clatter.

Dot lifted her head as she followed the noise and spied her friend. "Oh Gloria. You're back."

Gloria pasted a smile on her face and took a small step forward. "I was just coming in for a cup of coffee this morning..." Her voice trailed off. "What happened?"

Dot opened her mouth to speak but instead, she burst into tears. Gloria rushed over to the picnic table. She sat down on the edge of the bench and wrapped her arm around her friend's shoulders. "It's going to be alright, Dot. Don't worry."

Dot's shoulders sagged forward. She sobbed for several long moments before pulling herself together. Gloria stuck her hand in her purse and rummaged around inside. She pulled out a small pack of tissues, handed them to Dot, and waited as her friend pulled one of them from the package and blew her nose.

Ray patted his wife on the shoulder as he glanced worriedly toward the back door. "I better go inside and see what they're doing." He looked over at Gloria. "You'll be here for a few minutes?" He didn't want to leave his wife all alone, but he was anxious to see what, if anything, they were able to find.

Gloria nodded. "I'll stay out here 'til you get back." She watched as he disappeared inside the restaurant before turning to her friend. "What on earth happened?"

Dot drew a shaky breath, refusing to cave in to the overwhelming desire to start bawling again. "I-I'm not really sure. Everything was plugging along just fine when I came in this morning. I was doing my usual morning routine. Baking a batch of fresh cinnamon rolls for the coffee crowd, working on the chicken 'n dumplings." She paused. "You know, Wednesday is Dumpling Day."

How could Gloria forget Dumpling Day? Dot made the best chicken 'n dumplings in the entire Midwest. It was one of her busiest days of the week. People from the neighboring counties would drive miles just to taste Dot's delectable dumplings.

Gloria nodded. "Yes, of course. I love your dumplings."

Dot went on. "Well, the coffee crowd came and went. The place cleared out by 10:30 or so, which was a good thing." She grabbed another tissue and wiped her nose. "You know how some of those chatty folks can be. They like to sit around for hours and I have to keep running back and forth to the tables with pots of coffee while I'm trying to get ready for the lunch crowd."

Gloria nodded sympathetically. She knew some of the town folks were just lonely and Dot's was their unofficial hangout. It was hard on Dot, trying to keep up with them and prep for lunch.

Dot continued. "I was making good time. The dumplings were just right. I even made an extra batch. I had a hunch today was going to be extra busy."

"What time did Jennifer come in?" Gloria asked. Jennifer was Dot's part-time employee. She'd been working at the restaurant for a few months now.

It was a win-win situation for everyone. Jennifer's family was in a pinch money-wise. Her husband, Tony, had been working down at his dad's lumber mill trying to make ends meet. Work at the factory, his regular job, had slowed, and they had cut his hours. The extra tip money from waiting tables helped pay the bills.

Dot stared off, deep in thought. "Well... I think she got here right around eleven."

She went back to her story. "The lunch crowd started wandering in closer to 11:30. Jennifer and I had everything ready to go. Ray was in the back, firing up the grill and fryers."

Just then, Ray popped out from around the screen door. "Everything okay?" Gloria could see the concern etched on his face.

Dot turned a pair of red eyes to her husband. "Yeah, I'm doing alright. Just telling Gloria what happened."

He nodded. Without saying a word, he disappeared back inside.

Dot grabbed another tissue and dabbed at her eyes. *She must be getting to the bad part*, Gloria decided.

"By noon, the restaurant was packed. Jennifer and I were in front taking orders. Ray was back in the kitchen, frying away." She paused. "Funny thing, no one ordered the dumplings right away."

She glanced at Gloria. "Normally, they order the dumplings right off the bat."

"That does seem odd," Gloria agreed.

"It had to be close to half an hour before the first orders came. I fixed two heaping plates, added a bowl of biscuits, fresh from the oven, and carried them out front."

Gloria was curious. "Did you know the customers who ordered them?"

Dot shook her head. "It was a man and a woman. Their faces looked a little familiar. Like I've seen them before, but they're not regular customers."

Dot paused, her face started to pucker. The flow of tears threatened to begin again.

"Then what happened?" Gloria prompted. She couldn't bear to see her friend cry.

"I walked back in the kitchen. Jennifer was right behind me. She said something about the table I just served wanted talk to me."

Dot took a deep breath. "So I headed back out front. The woman. She pointed to the dumplings and said they smelled funny. Like, you know, chemically."

"What did you do then?"

"Well, I asked the man if his tasted okay. Apparently, he thought so. He kept eating and said they were fine."

She went on. "I took the woman's dish back to the kitchen with me. I made a small dish for myself, although I had tried them right after they finished cooking and they were good. But that was earlier," she added.

"What did the second dish taste like?" Gloria asked.

Dot made a sour face. "I don't know. All I know is it smelled terrible. That woman was right. There was something wrong."

She twisted the Kleenex around her finger as she fought to stay composed. "I hustled back to the dining room to take the dish from the man but it was too late."

Gloria sucked in a breath, waiting for what was coming next.

"By the time I got there, he was clutching at his throat. He whispered that his throat was on fire, right before he fell out of the chair and hit the floor," she said.

Gloria clutched her own throat. *How could something like this happen?*

Ray wandered back outside. He put a hand on Dot's shoulder and gently squeezed. "The police are gone now but I'm sure they will be back."

Dot whirled around to face her husband. "What about the man?"

Ray shook his head and shifted his gaze. "He didn't make it."

The color drained from Dot's face, her eyes stared blankly at her husband. "You mean he died?"

Ray nodded somberly. "I'm afraid so...on the way to the hospital."

Dot glanced over at Gloria. "Now what?"

Gloria didn't have an answer. The whole thing was surreal. Surely police would have the whole thing straightened out in no time. Dot's restaurant had been open for over a decade with nary a single restaurant inspection violation. No, this was either an accident – someone poured the wrong thing in the pot – or someone intentionally mixed poison in the food... but who and why?

Gloria glanced up at Ray. "What about the restaurant?"

He shook his head. "Closed down until the investigation is complete."

Dot gasped. Not run the restaurant? Where would all the people in town eat? Not only that, what would they think?

Her stomach churned violently. She clamped a hand over her mouth and darted over to the bushes that lined the edge of the patio.

Gloria felt helpless as she listened to the sounds of a woman's lifelong love and dreams shatter.

Dot loved that restaurant. It was her life...and Ray's life. The two had sunk their entire life savings into the place. It was all they had. It made her own stomach churn.

Dot fell back against the side of the restaurant. "I need to go home," she moaned. "I'm going to take a sleeping pill, crawl into bed and I'm not coming out until this is all over," she vowed.

"The car is out front," Ray reminded Dot. He turned to Gloria. "Can you give Dot a ride home? There's a crowd of people in front of the restaurant and I don't want her to have to deal with them."

Gloria nodded. "Yes, of course." She put her arm around Dot's shoulder and gently guided her down the alley toward the car.

Dot and Ray's house was a short drive from the restaurant. Gloria dropped her friend off, making sure she was safely inside and tucked into bed before she headed back into town.

She made a last minute decision to swing by Andrea's place. Andrea was Gloria's young friend. She was in the middle of a major renovation project on a fixer-upper home...a major fixer-upper. The old Johnson Mansion to be exact.

Gloria had stopped by the place several days earlier to check on the progress. The construction crew was moving right along, updating the electrical and plumbing inside so there wasn't much to see. Gloria was anxious to find out if the crew had started on the outside.

When she pulled in the drive, she spotted Andrea's sports car parked in the grass off to the side. She could see the crew was hard at work scraping away layers of peeling paint. It looked as if they had already replaced a large section of rotted boards on the front. In another week, Gloria guessed they would start painting, and she could hardly wait to see the finished product.

Gloria pulled Annabelle in next to the sports car. She slid out of the driver's seat and looked around. Andrea's blonde head was bent over a sawhorse. She was in deep conversation with a tall man wearing a hard hat. She hesitated, unsure whether she should interrupt.

Andrea must've sensed someone watching her. She looked up. Her lips curled in a welcoming smile. She held a finger up to the man, made her way over to her friend and then hugged Gloria tightly. "You made it back."

Gloria returned the hug. "Yes, and I'm glad to be home."

Andrea lowered her voice and glanced around. "I was in Dot's restaurant earlier having breakfast with the construction foreman when a man collapsed at one of the tables."

Gloria nodded. "It's a sad situation. I just dropped Dot off at home. She's really shook up."

Andrea shook her head sympathetically. "I know what she's going through." If anyone did, it would be Andrea. Police had charged Andrea with her husband's murder just over a year ago. That was how Andrea and Gloria had met...when Gloria helped solve the case and bring the real killer to justice. "Let me know if there's anything I can do to help," Andrea offered.

The construction supervisor was heading their way. "I have to finish up with him," she said. "Do you have a minute to come inside?"

"Absolutely," Gloria said. "It will help take my mind off poor Dot."

She waited out front while Andrea spent another few minutes with her head bent over the blueprints. She wandered around the side of the house to check the progress. The rest of the exterior was free of paint.

"Looks weird without paint, huh." Andrea stood beside her, gazing up at the side of her house. "Come back next week and the outside should be done."

"What color did you decide to paint it?" Gloria asked.

Andrea stuck her hand on hip and tilted her head. "You know, I'm torn between two colors. Traditional white with black shutters – or – what do you think of sunglow yellow with periwinkle blue shutters?"

Gloria knew what she would do. "Pick the one that makes you happy," she advised.

"I thought you would say that." Andrea grinned. "Yellow it is."

Gloria nodded her approval. She was a lot older than Andrea and it seemed like the older she got, the less she cared about not only appearances, but also what others thought. Life was too short to worry if someone didn't like yellow and periwinkle…

Andrea motioned her inside. "C'mon, I want to show you something."

Gloria followed Andrea up the narrow steps and in the back door.

It was nice to see a smile on her young friend's face. Last year had been nothing but sadness and heartache when Andrea's husband had been murdered. To make matters even worse, she discovered that he had been cheating on her.

Not long after that, the girls had found a body in the shed of the old Johnson mansion and Andrea was once again a suspect. Gloria and Andrea teamed up and tracked down the killers, in a roundabout way. Since then, things had settled down for Andrea and Gloria was relieved.

Gloria gasped as she stepped into the kitchen. The transformation was amazing. Shiny black granite covered the spacious countertops. The white oak cabinets had been restored to their original beauty.

Brand new state-of-the-art stainless steel appliances gleamed brightly. The kitchen was stunning...a blend of old and new. "It's beautiful," Gloria said.

Andrea's face beamed. "You think so? You really like it?"

Gloria shook her head. "No, I don't like it. I love it."

Andrea stepped over to the wall that divided the kitchen and the library on the other side. "How do you think it would look if I tore this wall down, opened this whole thing up and added a bar area?"

The kitchen was nice the way it was, but opening it up – well that would completely transform the rooms...make it more modern but retain a lot of the historic charm. Gloria slowly nodded. "I think that is a great idea. Did you think of that yourself?"

Andrea patted the flowered wallpaper. "Yep. The contractor told me this is not a load-bearing wall so they can take it out."

"I think you should become an interior designer. That's what I think," Gloria said.

"Really? Because that's what I was thinking myself. I'm having so much fun and have so many ideas."

If this was Andrea's dream, Gloria was behind her 100%. "Absolutely. In fact, when you're done with this, I'll hire you to help me with my place. It needs a bit of sprucing up," she added.

"Oh, no, Gloria. I love your farmhouse just the way it is." Andrea paused. "There are a few small things that would make it a little more functional..."

"Good. Then I'll be your first customer," Gloria told her.

Andrea shook her head. "But I don't want to charge you. You have helped me so much. I would do it as a favor."

Gloria shook her head firmly. "No, my dear. We can discuss that down the road if it's something you decide to do, but even friends need to get paid for their services."

"Knock, knock. Anyone home?" A male voice echoed from the front of the house.

"Oh, that must be Justin," Andrea said. "In here," she yelled back.

Gloria lifted a brow. "Justin?"

Andrea tucked a long strand of blond hair behind her ear. "He asked if he could stop by and see the place," she mumbled.

Justin was the mayor's son. He had taken a liking to Andrea the first time Gloria brought her to church. Gloria got the impression Andrea wasn't as keen on him, but maybe things had changed.

Justin's tall, lanky frame filled the doorway leading into the kitchen. He was holding a pizza box and a liter of Diet Coke. His eyes lit up when he saw Andrea. It took him a minute to realize Gloria was also in the room. "Ahem."

He turned his head, a twinge of color crept into his cheeks. "Hello Mrs. Rutherford."

"Hello Justin." Gloria turned to Andrea. "I'm going to head on out now."

"Would you like to have lunch with us?" Andrea asked.

Gloria shook her head. "Not this time, dear." She gave Andrea a small hug, smiled warmly at Justin and headed toward the front door.

As she got in the car, she thought of all that had changed in the past several months. Mostly for the better. Except for Dot. The whole thing was weighing heavy on Gloria's mind.

She started the car before glancing down at her cell phone, still resting in the center console. There was one missed call. It was her friend, Ruth.

Ruth was head postmaster at the post office in town. She was also Belhaven's unofficial snoop.

Ruth hadn't left a message, and Gloria could almost guarantee Ruth had called to find out what she knew about Dot's restaurant. She decided not to call her - or anyone else - until she had more information.

She didn't want anyone to think she was gossiping about the terrible incident, especially

Dot. She was certain she knew more about what had happened than anyone else, other than the police, that is.

Her plan would have worked out great if not for the fact that a bright yellow jeep she didn't recognize was parked in her driveway when she pulled in.   It was her friend, Lucy.

Gloria climbed out of her car. "What happened to your convertible?"

"I traded it in for something more practical." Lucy patted the hood of the jeep. "Now I'll have four wheel drive for the wintry roads."

Gloria peeked in the window. "Nice. I like it." She changed the subject. "You heard about Dot?"

"Yeah. I drove by there a little while ago. I saw your car parked at the end of the street," Lucy commented. "Did you talk to Dot?"

Gloria groaned inwardly. Lucy was in their small group of friends and she and Gloria were close. "Yeah. You want to come in for a cup of coffee?"

Lucy nodded. "I won't pry, although I know you know something," she said.

Gloria let out a sigh of relief and hugged her friend. "I appreciate that."

"But we can still talk about it?" Lucy asked.

Gloria nodded. "Sure."

Lucy followed her up the steps. "First, tell me about your trip to the mountains. Margaret said it was quite an adventure."

Gloria smiled. "That is an understatement." She stepped inside and headed to the counter and the coffee pot. "You might as well have a seat. You're not going to believe what happened."

After the coffee finished brewing, Gloria set two cups of coffee and a plate of baked goodies on the table before she filled Lucy in on all the details of the unexpected trip to the mountains, how they finally managed to track down Gloria's sister, Liz, and then found their long lost relative - Aunt Ethel.

The only part she left out was the part about finding the coins. That had to remain a secret until the three women – who made a pact to keep mum about the coins - were ready to share the news.

Lucy reached for a key lime tart. She peeled off the paper shell and took a small bite. "You have a long lost aunt?"

"Had." Gloria corrected her.

Lucy shook her bright mop of red curls as Gloria shared her story. "So I missed an awesome adventure..."

Gloria nodded. "Yep."

"That figures. No way could you go anywhere without having something crazy happen to you." Lucy snapped her fingers. "Do you still have your reward money socked away for that cruise next summer?"

Gloria nodded. During one of Gloria's last murder investigations, Lucy and she organized a late night stakeout at the old Johnson mansion. The stakeout turned into what could *possibly* have been considered a break-in at the old place. Of course, one could argue they didn't *technically* break in since the back door had been unlocked.

Lucy and Gloria stumbled upon some stolen money from a bank robbery and returned it to its rightful owner – the bank. There was a reward and each of them ended up with five thousand dollars.

The women decided to save the money for Lucy's dream vacation, a cruise, which was still in the planning stages.

The plan was to surprise their small group of friends – The Garden Girls – with an all-expenses paid cruise. In addition to Lucy and Gloria, there was Margaret, her friend who just returned from the Smoky Mountain trip, Dot and, last but not least, Ruth, the friend that ran the post office.

"Yeah, I stuck mine in a short-term CD. By the time it's ready to cash in, we will be ready to book the cruise," Gloria said.

Lucy grabbed a cream-filled donut before changing the subject. "What on earth happened over at Dot's?"

Lucy nibbled on her donut as Gloria explained how someone had died and that police had closed the restaurant until the investigation was completed.

Gloria didn't mention the poison in the dumplings since that hadn't been confirmed. She didn't want rumors flying around town.

Lucy finished the rest of her donut before taking a sip of coffee. She set it back down on the table. "We need to pray for her. This is just horrible."

Gloria agreed. The two friends bowed their heads and prayed a heartfelt prayer for their dear friend. "Dear Lord, we ask that you help investigators find the reason for the unfortunate incident at Dot's restaurant this morning and that Dot and Ray are cleared of all charges." Gloria paused. "And that they can re-open their restaurant because they need the money."

Lucy squeezed Gloria's hand. "Amen." She stood up. "I gotta get going. My washer is on the fritz and the repair guy is supposed to show up anytime now."

Gloria walked her to the door. She waved good-bye as she watched Lucy make her way to the jeep.

Back inside, she threw together a quick sandwich for lunch. Puddles and Mally stood next to each other and watched as Gloria placed slices of carved turkey on the bread.

"I know, I know, you want a bite." She grabbed two slices, dropped one in Mally's dish and the other in Puddles' dish. In one gulp, the pieces were gone.

She wrapped her sandwich in a paper towel and headed to the living room where she turned the TV on and to the weather station. It was time to start on her garden and she wanted to make sure the frost was out of the ground first.

She must have dozed off because when she woke, late afternoon soap operas were on. Her eyes darted to the clock. It was almost five already.

Gloria jumped out of the chair and headed to the bathroom. Paul would arrive in less than an hour to pick her up for their dinner date.

She jumped in the shower and lathered her hair with her favorite orange blossom-scented shampoo.

Her mind drifted to Dot as she spritzed on perfume. She wondered how Ray and she were holding up. She made a mental note to check on them after she finished getting ready.

She also wondered if Paul would be able tell her anything about the case. He was part of the Montbay County Sheriff's Department and his unit handled many of the investigations. It couldn't hurt to ask...

She let Mally out before she stepped back inside the kitchen and picked up the phone. She dialed Dot's home number. Ray picked up. "Hello?" he answered in a hushed tone.

"Hi Ray. Gloria here. I was just calling to see how Dot is holding up," she said.

Ray let out a long sigh. "I'm worried about her."

"That's what I was afraid of," Gloria fretted. She knew her friend was the ultimate worrywart. "I'm having dinner with Paul tonight. I'll see if he has any information he can tell me about the investigation."

"We would really appreciate that, Gloria." Ray paused. "Thank you for being such a good friend."

He lowered his voice again. "Seems like not everyone in Belhaven is such a loyal friend. You would not believe some of the phone calls we've gotten here at the house."

Gloria's heart went out to him. "People can be so ruthless and cruel, even so-called friends."

It saddened Ray to hear some of the comments, the thoughtless remarks about how they would never eat in the restaurant again because they would worry about being poisoned. Others told him they had gotten sick eating in the restaurant but never had the nerve to tell them, but looking back, maybe they should have...how the poor man might still be alive if they had spoken up.

Just the thought of the callous comments made him angry and bitter. He was glad Dot was still in bed. It would have destroyed her.

"Keep your chin up, Ray," Gloria encouraged. "We'll get through this and if there's anything I can do to help..."

Ray cut her off. "Maybe you can do a little poking around, see if you can get to the bottom of this."

Gloria had thought about it. She didn't want to stick her nose in where it didn't belong, but if Ray was asking her...

"I would be happy to see what I can find out," she said. "If you really want me to," she added.

Ray was relieved. That was exactly what he wanted. If anyone in this town could figure out what had happened to Dot's dumplings, it was Gloria. "You more than have my permission."

Gloria glanced out the window. She watched as Paul pulled in the drive. "Paul is here. I've got to go, but I'll get started on this first thing in the morning," she promised.

She hung up the phone and made her way to the door. Her heart skipped a beat as she watched the tall, handsome man – her man – make his way up the porch steps.

Gloria's hand flew to her chest when she spotted the bouquet of spring flowers he was carrying. She flung the door open and met him by the steps.

He opened his arms wide and Gloria stepped in as his arms closed around her.

She shut her eyes and breathed deeply. It was in that exact moment she realized just how

35

much she had missed him and how much he meant to her.

When she pulled away, there were tears in her eyes.

"I hope you're crying because you're happy to see me," he joked.

She half-hiccupped as she nodded her head. "Of course."

"These are for you." He held out the flowers. There were not only roses, but also her absolute favorite flower - yellow daisies.

"How did you know that daisies are my favorite?"

He shook his head. "I didn't, but I know you love yellow. I also noticed a small patch growing in the corner of the garden so I figured you must at least like them a little."

"Well, they are my favorite and they're beautiful," she exclaimed.

He trailed along behind her as she made her way back inside.

Gloria pulled an antique vase from the cupboard and arranged the flowers so the roses were in the center and the daisies lined the outside.

She set them in the center of the table before turning to Puddles, who was hovering nearby. "Don't you *dare* nibble on these flowers," she warned.

Puddles answered her by rubbing against her legs and meowing loudly.

Paul bent down and scratched his ears. He lifted his head and gazed at Gloria. "I heard about Dot's place. What a shame."

Gloria nodded. "It's just terrible. Poor Dot. She's taking this hard."

"I'm sure she is," Paul replied. "Right now, investigators don't have much to go on."

Gloria grabbed a light jacket off the hook by the door. Paul held the door for Gloria as she stepped onto the porch. She handed him her keys and waited as he locked up.

"There's a new restaurant I thought we could try. It's not too far from here and everyone I've talked to is giving it rave reviews."

A new restaurant – one that Gloria knew nothing about. She really was out of the loop. "What's the name?"

"Pasta Amore. It's over on Lakeshore Boulevard," he answered. "In Lakeville."

Lakeville was another small town but bigger than Belhaven. It was where Gloria's children attended school after they closed the small elementary school in Belhaven.

"Sounds perfect. I love Italian," Gloria said.

The two chatted easily as they drove to the restaurant. Gloria spent most of the time telling

Paul about her adventure in the mountains. When she got to the part where the three girls ended up in jail overnight, Paul started to say something but quickly closed his mouth.

Gloria held up her hand. "I know, I know. You told me someday I would end up in jail." She grinned. "I have to say, it really wasn't *that* bad."

She finished the rest of her story. The only part she left out was the part about the coins the girls found.

She felt a twinge of guilt for not telling all, but remembered her vow to Margaret and Liz. It wasn't like she was lying. She just wasn't telling him that part...at least not yet.

Although it was a weeknight, the restaurant parking lot was full. Maybe it was because many people from Belhaven decided to drive to Lakeville for dinner since Dot's wasn't open. A wave of guilt washed over her, as if she was betraying her friend for eating somewhere else...

A thought occurred to her. They were almost to the door when she stopped. "How long did you say this restaurant has been open now?"

He shrugged. "Not long. Maybe a week." It dawned on him why she had asked the question. "You don't think someone sabotaged Dot's place." It was a thought. A brand new restaurant opens, not far from an established competitor.

Could someone be ruthless enough to poison an innocent person, just to shut Dot's place down and take out the competition?

"Nothing should be ruled out," Gloria decided. This was the perfect place to start her investigation and she would start by finding out who owned Pasta Amore.

Gloria's detective radar shot up as she stepped inside and scanned the room. A few of the faces were familiar. Regulars at Dot's.

The hostess led them to a small corner table. The smell of freshly baked bread wafted from the kitchen.

They each ordered a glass of tea and sipped it as they studied the menu. Gloria tried to focus on the menu but her attention strayed toward the swinging doors that led to the kitchen. *If only she could find a way to get back there...*

When the waitress returned, Gloria turned her attention. "What a lovely restaurant," she complimented.

The girl smiled. "Thank you. We opened a few days ago."

"Wow. This place is already packed." She looked around. "The food must be to die for."

Paul gave her a hard look and slowly shook his head.

She smiled innocently before placing her order. "I'll have the baked lasagna, please."

Paul ordered a sampler trio and handed his menu to the waitress.

After she walked away, he turned to study his girlfriend. "You're not going to start tonight, are you?" He was wasting his breath. Gloria was already in sleuth mode.

She lowered her gaze. "I can't help myself," she admitted. and then silently vowed to put the investigation on the back burner and focus on Paul.

For a while it worked. Their dinner arrived and everything looked delicious. Gloria's mouth began to water as she lifted a forkful of pasta to her lips.

The lasagna sauce had just the right amount of tang and plenty of gooey cheese loaded on top.

She didn't want to like this place, but she did. If not for Dot's, she would definitely return.

The waitress returned to pick up their dirty plates. "The lasagna was delicious," Gloria said. "My compliments to the chef."

The girl smiled as she juggled the dirty plates. "I'll be sure to pass your praise on..."

"Who is the chef...the owner?" Gloria fished. She just couldn't help herself. She had to know who owned the place.

The girl nodded. "Yes. He and his wife moved here not long ago. They owned an upscale pizza place in Chicago," she explained.

"Oh really? I wonder if I have ever been to their restaurant. What did you say the name of it was?"

Gloria knew the girl hadn't said. She sucked in her breath, hoping the girl remembered the name.

"I think the name was Amici Trattoria, or something like that. It was somewhere near the

43

Magnificent Mile." She shrugged. "That's all I know."

"Well, it was delicious and I'm sure they will be successful here."

Paul didn't bother commenting. He knew it was useless. He also knew Gloria would do whatever she could to help her friend, not that he could blame her. Time and again she proved she was good at solving mysteries and if anyone could use a little help right now, it was Dot.

Gloria snuggled next to Paul on the drive back to the farm. She felt like a teenager as she slid across the seat and closed the distance between them.

He lifted his arm and she placed her head against his side as they chatted about his job. Paul had been tossing around the idea of retiring.

"What are you going to do with yourself when you have all that free time?" she asked.

Paul had a farm, too. His was slightly larger than her place, and he leased the surrounding farmland to farmers during growing season.

The house was older and needed some updating. He wasn't getting any younger and soon, projects of a certain size would be too much for him to take on.

The more he thought about it, the more he decided it was time to turn in his badge. His pension would more than carry him through his retirement years. Plus, he had been dabbling in the stock market for a while now and his investments were turning a tidy profit.

He glanced down at Gloria's head. If Gloria and he continued on this path and things grew more serious, he wondered what they would do with two big old farmhouses.

Paul knew she loved her home but it needed some work, just like his. In his mind, there was no sense in keeping two farms. It was

45

something he had been mulling over, but every time he got to the part about who would have to give up what, he reached a standstill.

Gloria could see the top of Mally's head peeking through the kitchen door's glass windowpane as they pulled in the drive. After the trip to the Smoky Mountains and taking Mally along, the dog was determined to go everywhere Gloria went.

Paul walked her to the door and waited while she unlocked it. "Do you have time to come in for a piece of key lime dessert or cup of coffee?"

He shook his head. "I'd like nothing more but I have the early shift tomorrow."

She wasn't ready to give up. "What about dinner later this week?" she asked hopefully. "I can throw a couple steaks on the grill."

"You do owe me a steak dinner," he teased. "That sounds good."

Paul nodded his head and then gently kissed Gloria on the lips.

She wrapped her arms around his neck, surprising even herself when she pulled him closer.

The kiss lasted several long seconds. By the time they broke free, Gloria's heart was racing and her breathing was more than a little uneven.

"Many more kisses like that and we will have to start bringing a chaperone along," he joked.

Gloria blushed, just a little this time. "Maybe it's a good thing you're not coming inside, after all."

Before he could change his mind and throw all caution to the wind, he gave her one last peck on the lips, a quick hug and then turned to go.

After he was gone, Gloria hung her jacket on the hook by the door and set her purse on the table.

Mally tapped the door with her bandaged paw. Gloria lifted the paw and studied the bandage still covering the gunshot wound.

It appeared to be healing quite nicely. Still, Gloria wasn't taking any chances. Mally had an appointment with the vet the next day and Gloria hoped the vet would give them a clean bill of health.

Gloria sat on the edge of the steps as she watched Mally prance around the yard, sniffing a little of this, watering a little of that.

The sun had set hours ago and the moon was high in the sky. It seemed bright...brighter than normal for this time of year. It was almost as bright as a fall harvest moon.

Her mind wandered to the restaurant. What was the name of the place in Chicago?

Amichis? Armandos? No, that wasn't it. *Amici Trattoria.*

She jumped to her feet. "C'mon Mally. Let's head back inside."

Gloria jotted the name on a slip of paper next to her computer and then headed to the bathroom to get ready for bed. Tomorrow was shaping up to be another busy day.

Chapter Two

First thing the next morning, Gloria called Dot's home phone. This time, Dot answered. "Hi Gloria."

Gloria could tell by the tone of her friend's voice there was no good news but she decided to ask anyway. "Have you heard anything from the police?"

"No. Ray just left to go meet them at the restaurant. I guess they want to do one more search of the place."

"They haven't cleared the restaurant so you can open back up?"

"No." Dot paused. "I'm not sure I even want to, Gloria. People are saying some really mean things."

Gloria could tell her friend was on the verge of breaking down and it broke her heart.

"Don't listen to one word of that Dorothy Jenkins," Gloria scolded. "Anyone who said one bad word is no friend of yours – of ours – and they're just jealous." It took a lot to get Gloria ticked off but this was getting her all fired up.

When I find out who the trash talkers are, Gloria vowed silently, *I will personally set them straight.*

Dot talked for a few more minutes before telling Gloria she felt sick to her stomach and needed to go lay down.

Gloria stared at her silent phone. The call made Gloria even more determined to get to the bottom of the poisoning and to help clear Dot's and Ray's good name.

She strode over to the computer. It was time to find out more about the owners of Amici Trattoria in Chicago.

Gloria found the restaurant online, found the location; she even found all the raving reviews. What she couldn't find was the owner's name. She tried searching the property appraiser's office and the county assessor's office and came up empty-handed.

Frustrated, she shut off the computer. She stomped over to the kitchen door, grabbed Mally's leash and her jacket off the hook. "C'mon, girl. Let's go for a walk."

Mally and Gloria walked the property and the fields. They wandered down to the creek on the other side of the property.

Gloria sat on the edge of the bank as Mally frolicked near the water. The serene spot helped soothe her frustration and she felt better. The fresh country air helped clear her head.

Gloria glanced at her watch. Mally's vet appointment was in an hour. She jumped to her feet. "Mally, we gotta go." They made a mad dash for the keys and the car.

Rain began falling as they drove down Main Street Belhaven, past Dot's Restaurant. The police tape was gone but the place was empty except for a police car and Ray's van. She could see Ray standing by the front window. He was inside talking to a police officer.

She offered up a quick prayer for Dot and Ray, and asked for help in solving the mystery.

The vet visit was quick and easy. He gave Mally a clean bill of health, told Gloria the wound was healing nicely and that there would only be a small scar as a reminder of the entire incident.

The vet lifted Mally off the examination table and set her down on all fours. "How did your dog get shot?"

Gloria sighed as she shook her head. "It's a long story and you wouldn't believe me, even if I told you."

The young vet walked Gloria to the front reception desk. "You have a reputation around

these parts for being a super-sleuth." He tapped
his bottom lip with his index finger. "Let me
guess. It had something to do with one of your
mysteries."

Gloria grinned. "Yeah, you could say
that."

He knelt down and rubbed Mally's ears.
"I'm sure you were some sort of hero dog and
that's how you got shot," he guessed.

"You would be 100% right."

He set Mally's chart on the reception desk.
"We don't charge super-hero dogs so today was a
freebie."

Gloria never intended to get out of paying
for the visit. She started to open her purse. "But
I don't mind..."

He shook his head firmly. "Please. I
insist."

She shut her purse and grabbed Mally's leash. "Thank you so much." She paused when she reached the door. "I haven't found a vet for Mally. If you have room for her, we would like to start coming here."

He grinned. "We would love to have you." He bent down to Mally-level. "You too."

Gloria and Mally made their way out to Annabelle and climbed inside. On the drive home, she decided to check in with Ruth at the post office.

She didn't want her friend to think she was avoiding her. In addition, Ruth was the only Garden Girl Gloria hadn't seen since returning from the mountains.

Ruth was waiting on a customer inside the lobby. She spotted Gloria as soon as she stepped through the door.

Ruth grabbed a book of stamps from the drawer and shoved them across the counter at the woman.

The woman made her way to the side counter and began working on a stack of envelopes. She peeled a stamp from the pack and carefully centered it in the corner of the first envelope.

Ruth stomped over to where the woman was standing. "Here, let me help you with that." She didn't wait for a reply. Instead, she grabbed the pile of envelopes and snatched the book of stamps from the woman's hands.

Ruth peeled a stamp out of the book and slapped it on the corner of the envelope before stamping the next one in the stack.

The poor woman just stared at Ruth, too stunned to respond.

Gloria clamped her hand over her mouth to stifle a giggle.

Ruth finished the pile in seconds flat. She picked up the pile of envelopes, handed the book of stamps to the woman and then walked her to the door. "Have a nice day."

The woman was still staring at Ruth as she walked out.

Ruth closed the door behind her and spun around to face Gloria. "That man in Dot's restaurant was poisoned."

Gloria didn't have the heart to tell her she already knew that. "What a shame."

"We need a Garden Girls meeting. Maybe if we put our heads to together, we can figure out how on earth something like this happened," Gloria suggested.

Ruth nodded. "I think you're right. Where can we meet now that Dot's place is out of commission – at least for now?"

Ruth went on. "I tried calling Dot's house earlier and no one answered." She lowered her voice. "Ray said she's depressed and refuses to get out of bed."

Gloria was afraid that was going to happen. "I'll run over to Dot's right now, tell her we're having a meeting and she has to be there." She paused. "Let's do it tomorrow at noon – on your lunch break. We can meet at my house," she added.

Chapter Three

Gloria headed out the door and drove straight to Dot's house. Ray's truck was gone but Dot's van was in the drive.

Gloria hopped out of the car and headed to the front door. The curtains were drawn tight. *Maybe she went somewhere with Ray*, Gloria thought.

Gloria pressed the doorbell. She waited for several long seconds before she pressed it a second time.

She could have sworn the front curtain moved. "Dot. It's Gloria. Are you in there?" she hollered through the crack in the door.

When she heard a small *thump,* she knew Dot was inside. She pounded her fist on the metal frame. "Dot. I know you're in there."

Gloria crossed her arms, determined to wait her out. She stood there a good five minutes before the front door opened a fraction of an inch. Gloria stuck her nose in the crack, her eyeball pressed close to the metal doorjamb. "Let me in, Dot. Please..." she pleaded.

The door swung open and Gloria gasped at the sight of her friend. She had never seen Dot in such a state of disarray.

The thing that shocked Gloria the most was the expression on her face. It was a look of utter despair. Before Dot could change her mind, Gloria squeezed inside.

She decided her best approach was to act as if everything was perfectly normal, that there was nothing unusual about her friend wearing her bathrobe in the middle of the afternoon...with no makeup on and her hair matted to the side of her head.

"We're having a Garden Girls meeting tomorrow at noon. You need to come," she said.

Dot shook her head. "I can't." She waved her arm towards the kitchen. "Follow me."

Gloria followed her friend to the kitchen. Dot flipped on the light switch just inside the door and Gloria's jaw fell.

The kitchen was a disaster. Dirty dishes filled the sink. The trashcan was overflowing. A moldy, half-eaten sandwich was on the table, along with a jug of milk.

Gloria placed the palm of her hand against the side of the milk carton. It was warm. She unscrewed the cap and took a whiff.

Gloria wrinkled her nose at the overpowering stench of sour milk. She pushed the carton from her face. "This milk is sour."

Gloria plugged her nose as she poured the semi-solid substance down the kitchen sink.

Dot pulled out a kitchen chair and plopped down at the table. She acted as if she hadn't heard a word Gloria had said as she stared blankly into space.

Gloria pulled out a chair and slid it close Dot's chair. She waved a hand in front of her friend's face. "Earth to Dot. Are you in there?"

Still no response.

Gloria snapped her fingers. "Dot," she yelled.

That seemed to do the trick. Dot shook her head. "I'm sorry, Gloria. I was a million miles away."

Gloria leaned forward, her face just inches from Dot's face. "We're having a Garden Girls meeting tomorrow at noon at my place. You have to come."

Dot shook her head and her eyes filled with tears. "I can't. I'm too depressed."

"That's exactly why you have to come," Gloria argued. "You need to snap out of this.

You're not helping yourself or your restaurant by hiding out in your house."

"I-I give up," Dot whispered. "My life is over."

"Dot Jenkins, your life is NOT over. You're a fighter. We're going to figure out how that man was poisoned at your restaurant and you're going to help us," Gloria vowed.

Dot clutched the edge of her robe in her fist. "You really think we can?"

Gloria reached over and squeezed her friend's arm. "Without a doubt and we're starting tomorrow." She jumped to her feet. "I'll be here at 11:30 to pick you up."

Before Dot could protest, Gloria headed to the front door.

***

Gloria woke early the next morning. Since the Garden Girls meeting was at her place, she needed to whip up some tasty treats for her guests. A light lunch was in order, she decided.

She spent the morning preparing a large tray of finger sandwiches...tuna, roast beef and chicken salad, along with some chips and homemade salsa she had made a few weeks ago. For dessert, it would be butterscotch parfaits and frosted sugar cookies.

She mixed a batch of iced tea before setting the table.

Half an hour before the girls were scheduled to arrive, she darted out to her lilac bush and snipped the ends of a few of the purple flowers before arranging them in a small vase.

She slid the arrangement to the center of the kitchen table and right next to the bouquet of flowers Paul had brought her. The room smelled heavenly with the scent of lilac that filled the air.

Gloria puttered the last few minutes, moving this and straightening that. She was wound tighter than a top. Her anxiety wasn't from having the girls over for lunch, although that was a bit stressful. She was distracted with Dot's dilemma.

When everything was in place, she hopped in the car and headed to Dot's house. On the way, Gloria said a quick prayer for Dot.

She let out a sigh of relief when she pulled into Dot's drive. Dot's van was in the driveway and the front living room curtains were open.

Gloria slid out of the car and made her way up the steps. She reached out to ring the doorbell, but before her finger touched the buzzer, the door swung open.

Dot stood before her looking like her normal self. Her hair was done, make-up in place and she was wearing a cheerful spring outfit. She pushed the screen door open to let Gloria in.

Gloria hugged her friend. "You look like a ray of sunshine," she exclaimed.

Dot smiled but the smile didn't reach her sorrow-filled eyes. Dot returned the hug for a brief moment before pulling back. "Thanks for coming to get me, Gloria."

She grabbed her purse off the end table and followed Gloria out the front door.

On the short ride back to Gloria's, the girls made small talk, careful to avoid the elephant in the car – the dead customer.

Gloria unlocked her backdoor and led Dot into the kitchen. It was still hard to accept the fact that nowadays she had to lock her doors every time she went somewhere.

She poured Dot a fresh cup of coffee and started to sit down at the table when she spied Ruth's van pull in, followed by Lucy's snazzy new jeep, the top down.

Gloria grinned when she spied Margaret in the passenger seat, a bright blue scarf tied 'round her head.

The women made their way across the drive and up the steps. Gloria stepped outside to greet them. It was nice to have them all together again.

The girls settled in around the table. Gloria grabbed her Bible from the small stand in the corner. A particular verse had been stuck in her head and she knew the Lord wanted her to share it with Dot as a reminder. "The Lord gave me this verse for you, Dot." She opened her Bible and read Romans 8:28 (KJV):

> *"And we know that all things work together for good to them that love God, to them who are the called according to his purpose."*

Dot dabbed at her eyes with the sleeve of her shirt. "Thanks Gloria. I needed to hear that."

Gloria closed the Bible and set it on the stand behind her before passing around the tray of sandwiches.

Dot grabbed a tuna wedge and roast beef slider before passing the tray to Ruth. After the girls loaded their lunch plates, they bowed their heads in prayer.

"Dear Heavenly Father, we thank you for this food. We thank you for the time you've given us to spend together as friends and we pray, Lord, that you'll help us clear our dear friend Dot's name and figure out how that poor man ended up getting poisoned in her restaurant. We say a special prayer for his family." She finished the prayer with, "Thank you for Your Son, Jesus, and our salvation. In Jesus name."

"Amen," the group echoed.

The girls munched on their sandwiches, each of them declaring them the best they had ever tasted.

They chatted about Gloria and Margaret's trip to the mountains to track down Liz. When Gloria got to the part about Mally's shooting, the dog must have heard her name.

She wandered out into the kitchen to check for floor scraps and for a little attention. Mally made her way around the table as each of the girls patted her head and praised her for being such a loyal companion and hero.

Ruth was the first to ask the question Gloria knew was coming. "So what happened with the treasure? Did you find anything?" All eyes were on Gloria now, including Margaret's.

Gloria remembered the vow to keep silent about the coins until all three women agreed to talk and they were certain the coins were theirs for the keeping.

She answered as honestly as she could without giving anything away. "We found something but we're not sure of the value or if we will get to keep what we found."

Margaret added. "We decided until we're certain what we found is ours to keep, we're keeping a lid on it."

That seemed to satisfy the girls' curiosity, at least for the moment.

Ruth changed the subject. "It's almost time to start up with visits to the town's shut-ins. Since we don't have anything from our gardens yet, what do you think about taking some baked goods – you know breads, rolls, cakes. Stuff like that..."

Gloria nodded. They had slacked off a little through the winter. Partly for lack of people to visit and partly because of bad weather and slippery roads.

Now that spring had arrived, it was time to start the visits again. "I'll be happy to bake some bread," she offered. "Who is homebound?"

All eyes turned to Ruth. Ruth was the one person in town who knew what was going on since she ran the post office. On top of that, Ruth made it a point to stick her nose into everyone's business, at least the ones that would let her.

"Millie Tate just had a hip replacement. She's not going to be able to get out for quite some time. We should add her to the list for at least the next month."

Lucy clucked. "Oh, that poor thing. I remember the day she fell on the ice trying to get to her mailbox last winter. She was out there a good hour before someone drove by and noticed her sprawled out in her driveway."

They all agreed Millie was on the list until further notice.

"Anyone else?" Margaret asked Ruth.

Ruth grimaced. "There is one more..."

"Who?" Gloria asked. Whoever it was, Ruth wasn't keen on mentioning, judging by the tone of her voice.

"Judith Arnett," Ruth said. "She was trying to shoo a stray cat out of her yard and she fell into a hole. She twisted her ankle and is on crutches for the next few weeks," she added.

The room grew silent. It was so quiet; you could have heard a pin drop.

Judith Arnett was one of the most unlikeable residents in Belhaven. She and her small band of cronies carried on as if they owned the town.

Judith made it her personal mission to spread mean, malicious rumors. Her main objective? To ruin innocent peoples' lives – and reputations.

Just last month, she spread a hateful rumor about Gus Smith. Gus and his wife, Mary Beth, owned a small automotive shop on the edge of town. She told anyone that would listen that she caught him drinking out behind his shop during business hours.

The rumor spread like wildfire and Gus's business dropped like a rock. When Mary Beth caught wind of the malicious rumor Judith had started, she marched right over to Judith's place and gave her a piece of her mind.

Gloria would have given anything to witness the exchange. Mary Beth was as sweet as sugar until you crossed her. It was then the fiery Italian temper bubbled over and woe to whoever might be on the receiving end.

Next thing Gloria knew, Judith was keeping a low profile, avoiding the shops in town like the plague. Gloria had even heard a rumor she was taking her mail to nearby Green Springs just so she wouldn't chance a run in with Mary Beth.

"If you're going to visit Judith, you can count me out," Dot announced.

Dot was never one to judge people – always the first to forgive, even if someone had

73

wronged her. For Dot to refuse to visit Judith was a surprise...

All eyes turned to Dot. She had been quiet so far, and with everything going on, no one could blame her...

"I caught her stealing from the restaurant last week and kicked her out," Dot told the group.

It was the first any of them had heard about the theft. Judith wasn't the nicest of people – but a thief?

"She stopped in for breakfast with a couple of her cronies the other day. After they paid at the cash register, Judith's friends left but Judith headed toward the restroom in the back."

Dot continued. "I was still behind the cash register when she came out. When she walked by me, I noticed her purse was bulging open and I could see inside."

Ruth leaned forward. "What did she take?"

"Instead of using the restroom, she must have snuck into the kitchen. I asked to see what she had inside her purse. At first she refused, but when Ray came over to see what was going on, she changed her mind."

"And?" Lucy nudged.

"She was trying to steal the small espresso machine from the kitchen."

The girls gasped in horror. *Judith – a thief?*

"I took the machine back and told her she was never to step foot in our restaurant again," Dot finished.

"When was that?" Gloria asked.

Dot paused for a moment as she thought about it. "Just the other day. I think last Saturday." She shrugged.

"Right before the poisoning," Margaret pointed out.

Lucy drummed her fingers on the tabletop. "You don't think she came back and poisoned your dumplings to get even..."

"How could she?" Dot wondered. "I banned her from the restaurant."

The whole conversation got Gloria to thinking. Dot's kitchen was in the back.

Every time Gloria had ever gone into Dot's kitchen, the back door was wide open and the screen door unlocked. With all the ovens and equipment running, the kitchen got hot.

In the warmer months, especially the spring and summer, they left the door open to cool it.

Was it possible someone snuck into the restaurant just long enough to put something in the dumplings and then sneak back out?

Gloria wasn't the only one thinking the exact same thing.

"After you made the dumplings, did you leave the kitchen?" Ruth asked. "You know, run any errands between the time the dumplings were made and the first dish left the kitchen?"

Dot grew thoughtful. So much had happened and her brain wasn't functioning properly. "I'm not sure..."

Gloria pulled her chair close to Dot. "Think hard, Dot. This is important."

"Well, after I made the chicken and dumplings, I did a quick check of the supply closet. Wednesday, after close, is our day to refill the salt and pepper shakers and all the other table condiments," Dot explained.

Her forehead crinkled. "Yes. I did leave the restaurant. Ray was in the front talking to Officer Joe Nelson. We were low on salt and we weren't getting another delivery until Friday so I hung up my apron and headed out the front door." She went on. "I ran down to the Quick Stop grocery on the corner..."

"So no one was in the back – at least for a few minutes," Lucy said.

Dot shook her head. "No. Both Jennifer and Ray were in the front when I left the restaurant."

Gloria twisted her earring thoughtfully. "Which would give someone enough time to slip in through the back screen door, dump something in the dumplings and then sneak back out without being seen."

Gloria grabbed a pad of paper and pen from her junk drawer. She plopped down, scribbled "Suspects" at the top of the sheet and underlined it.

She wrote the number "1" and put Judith Arnett's name beside it. Halfway down the page, she started another line titled, "Witnesses."

Gloria turned to Dot. "Who was in the restaurant Wednesday morning that you remember? I think we should question them."

"Officer Nelson because Ray was talking to him. Andrea was there. She was sitting at a table in the back with a man wearing work boots and construction-type clothes," Dot said. "She ordered my favorite breakfast - biscuits and sausage gravy," she added.

Gloria scribbled furiously. "Anyone else you can remember?"

"Judith's husband, Carl, was in there with Al Dickerson."

Ruth changed the subject. "Did you hear about the new restaurant that opened in Lakeville a week or so ago?"

"You mean Pasta Amore?" Gloria asked.

Lucy nodded. "Someone mentioned it to me the other day, that they have authentic Italian food." She glanced at poor Dot. "I'm sure Dot's food is a hundred times better than that place," she added.

Dot's face fell. "So that's where everybody is eating now that my place is closed."

Margaret rubbed her chin. "Maybe it's the new restaurant owners and they are trying to sabotage Dot's place," she said.

Gloria grabbed the pot of coffee and refilled the cups, and then made her rounds with glasses of iced tea. "That's what I was thinking, but they're only open for dinner and Dot's is open for breakfast, lunch *and* dinner."

"Maybe they plan on expanding their hours," Ruth suggested.

Gloria set the pitcher of tea back on the counter. "We need to look into that."

Ruth glanced at her watch. "I gotta get back to work. My lunch break is almost over." She grabbed a couple sugar cookies and her purse before heading to the door. "I'll keep my ear to the ground, you know, see if anyone is talking." She looked at Dot. "Don't worry. We're going to get to the bottom of this no matter what," she promised.

With that, Ruth bolted out the door and hustled to her van. Gloria watched as she peeled out of the driveway and headed toward town. She glanced at the clock.

Ruth had one minute to spare before the post office was scheduled to reopen. Judging by the way that she tore out of the drive, she might just make it.

"Are you going to check out the new restaurant?" Lucy asked.

Gloria turned to Dot. "You want to take a ride over there...see what we can find out?" She didn't dare tell Dot that Paul and she had eaten at Pasta Amore the other night. It almost seemed like a betrayal to admit she had.

"I-I guess so..." Dot said. She looked at Margaret and Lucy.

Margaret shook her head. "As much as I would like to, I have a meeting with a financial adviser later today." She gave Gloria a quick look. The look meant Margaret was meeting with an adviser to discuss what they could do with any windfall they might come into if the coins turned out to be as valuable as everyone thought.

Gloria nodded. "Margaret is out then." She turned to Lucy. "You want to come along?"

Lucy grabbed a butterscotch parfait, stuck a spoon inside the cup and scooped out a large spoonful of sweet creaminess. She popped it in her mouth thoughtfully. "Mmm. This is *so* good."

She scooped another spoon before she glanced at the clock on the wall. "I have to be back by four. Bill is taking me to the gun range for target practice."

Gloria stuck her hand on her hip. "As much skeet shooting, squirrel hunting and other creature killings you two do, I would think you would be a pro by now."

Lucy stuck the spoon in her mouth and shook her head. "Nope. I'm not very good at all," she admitted.

"Maybe next time." Gloria said. "Are you up for it, Dot?"

"You really should go," Margaret urged her. "It's not good for you to stay shut up in that house twenty four hours a day."

Dot grabbed a parfait cup and then reached for a cookie. She dipped the cookie in the pudding and took a big bite. She chewed on it for a long moment. "Yeah. I guess I should. If we don't figure out who poisoned the pot - who will?"

Gloria covered the leftover sandwiches and shoved them in the fridge, along with the remaining butterscotch desserts before she grabbed her purse and headed to the door.

Mally heard the jingle of Gloria's keys and followed her to the door. Gloria bent down. "Sorry girl. We have to go without you this time. I don't think a fancy Italian restaurant will allow dogs inside."

Mally dropped her head and slunk over to her bed in the corner. She gave Gloria a sad face before she flopped down on the bed and closed her eyes.

Lucy patted Gloria's arm. "She will be okay. I think you've spoiled that dog rotten."

Gloria sighed. It was true. Mally was spoiled, but in a good way. After all, what was wrong with the dog wanting to be with her?

She gave Mally one last glance before she followed the girls outside and shut the door.

Margaret tied the bright blue scarf around her head and followed Lucy to the jeep. "Keep us posted if you manage to find any good clues."

Dot and Gloria watched Lucy's jeep roar out of the driveway before climbing into Annabelle.

Chapter Four

The drive to Lakeville took a quick half an hour. On the way, Dot and Gloria talked about the weather, their grandkids...anything but the death.

As they got close to town, Gloria had a thought. "Maybe we should talk to Jennifer. You know, find out if she noticed anything odd or anyone unusual lurking around the other morning."

Gloria was certain the police had already talked to the part-time employee. Perhaps they had missed something.

Dot had planned to talk to Jennifer. She just didn't have it in her to call her yet. With the restaurant shut down, there was a chance that Jennifer was going to quit. Who would want to work for someone that poisoned people? "Yeah, I guess so."

Gloria glanced at Dot. "Leave it to me," Gloria said. "I'll get ahold of her."

Dot was relieved. "Could you?" Tears welled up in her eyes. She wiped them away with the back of her hand. "I don't know what to say to her...or anyone else."

It was the least Gloria could do for her friend. "I'll call her tomorrow," she promised.

The restaurant was in downtown Lakeville, right off the main road. They slowed as they passed by the front. The new owners had remodeled the exterior.

The building had originally been built as a boarding house for the men who constructed the railroad that ran through town.

For years, it sat vacant until a local resident decided to fix it up and turn it into a drugstore. It stayed that way until the owner retired. The owner's children weren't interested in living in Lakeville and once again, the place sat vacant for a long time, up until a few months ago when the mysterious new owners from Chicago remodeled it and turned it into the restaurant.

Gloria pulled into an empty spot in front of the building. Her heart sank as she read the sign. The restaurant wouldn't open for another hour.

Dot was disappointed. "I guess we should have called first."

Gloria shook her head. "Let's head around back. I'm sure someone is inside getting ready for the dinner rush."

The girls climbed out of the car, walked around the side of the building and headed for the alley in the rear.

Gloria spied three vehicles parked off to the side. One of them was a shiny, new SUV with an Illinois license plate.

Gloria slipped her glasses on. She grabbed her phone from her purse and switched it to camera mode. She stepped close to the SUV and leaned forward to snap a picture of the license plate thinking that maybe she could track down the restaurant owner using the license plate number.

Dot took a step toward Gloria. "What are you doing?" she whispered loudly.

Just then, the back door of the restaurant swung open. A short, dark-haired man stepped onto the stoop. "What is going on back here?" he said in a loud voice.

Gloria jerked up. The pocket of her sweater caught on the trailer hitch. She tried to yank it free but the sweater refused to budge. Her head bobbed up and down as she tried in vain to pull herself free.

The man must have wondered what in the world was going on. He hopped off the steps and made his way to the back of the vehicle. At that precise moment, Gloria's sweater ripped free.

She stumbled backwards and landed on her rear, the cell phone still clutched in the palm of her hand.

Dot reached down and helped Gloria to her feet. "We here – uh – admiring..." Her voice trailed off.

She tried again. "We were admiring the color of the building and I, uh. I was telling my friend that I wanted to paint my house the same color."

Dot gave Gloria a hard stare. "So – uh, she offered to take a picture. That's when she dropped her phone."

The man gave them an odd look and then shrugged his shoulders.

Gloria quickly changed the subject. "The new owners did a nice job remodeling the old place," she said.

The man smiled. "Thanks." He shoved his hands in his pockets and looked up at the restaurant. "My wife and I have been working on it for a couple months."

"The restaurant is only open for dinner?" Dot blurted out.

"Yes, but starting Saturday we will be open for breakfast and lunch, too. Other than a fast food joint down the road, we're the only restaurant in the area," he explained.

Dot started to tell him "no they weren't" but she bit her tongue. She didn't want him to know who she was. Now that he was close, she was able to get a good look at this face. He looked familiar, as if she had seen him somewhere before...

Gloria could tell Dot wanted to say something - something she would regret. She grabbed Dot's hand and started to pull her away. "We'll have to come back and try it." She gave a small wave before hurrying off.

Dot marched along beside Gloria. "Did you hear that?" she huffed. "He's going to start serving breakfast and lunch." She mimicked his voice. "I think he poisoned my food. Somehow he snuck into my restaurant and dumped something in my dumplings."

"I know you're upset Dot but we can't jump to conclusions. We need to do more investigating," Gloria said. "Remember Judith? She has motive, too."

"True." Dot stomped her foot. "It's so dang frustrating."

The girls rounded the corner of the building and made their way over to Annabelle. They climbed inside before Gloria answered. "We need to be patient, Dot. Even if it means the restaurant stays closed a little longer."

Dot stared down at her hands. There were moments she wished it would just stay closed forever and there were others, she wanted desperately to be back at work. Back in her kitchen doing what she loved – feeding people and making them happy. "I know. It's just hard."

Gloria turned the car on and backed into the street. "Someone committed a murder and that someone is still roaming the streets."

"And that someone is trying to frame me," Dot pointed out. "That guy from the restaurant. He looks familiar. Like I've seen him somewhere before..."

"I'm sure he has eaten at your restaurant," Gloria guessed. "You know, checking out the competition and all."

"Tomorrow I'll talk to Jennifer," Gloria promised. "I'll do a little digging around to see what I can find out about Mr. Pasta Amore."

Gloria was relieved to find Ray at home when she dropped Dot off in the drive. She knew that there had been a lot for Dot to digest and until they solved the murder, things weren't going to get any easier for her.

Gloria glanced at the clock. Paul was working the night shift again. She remembered his promise to come over for a steak dinner. If she was lucky, maybe she could wheedle a little info out of Paul about the investigation, like the type of poison the killer had used.

Chapter Five

Gloria spent a restless night worrying about Dot, wondering about Judith and trying to figure out when she could fit a second dinner at Pasta Amore into her schedule.

She could ask Margaret to go with her. That way, she could kill two birds with one stone. Do a little detective work on the case and talk to Margaret one-on-one about the coins, which reminded her of something else.

It was her job to contact several attorneys about setting up wills in case they did have million dollar coins.

Gloria crawled out of bed bright and early the next morning. Her first order of business was to let Mally out for a run.

She grabbed the list of witnesses that were in the restaurant the morning of the poisoning.

Carl Arnett and Al Dickerson were at the top of the list.

Gloria scratched Carl Arnett off her list. No way did she want to chance a run in with Judith. The woman had lowered to a new level in Gloria's book, what with her trying to steal from Dot.

She slipped her reading glasses on and grabbed the telephone book. The listing for Belhaven wasn't long. There were no more than 900 people in the whole town and she had no problem finding the phone number for Al Dickerson.

She picked up the phone and dialed the number, still not certain what she should say. Gloria was much better at winging it.

"Hello?"

"Uh. Hi Al. This is Gloria Rutherford." She paused. "Uh, I was wondering if it would be possible for me to stop by your place sometime today. I heard you were in Dot's on Wednesday when that man was poisoned."

"Yeah, it was just terrible. Keeled over, right there at the table," he said. "His wife was hysterical. Poor thing."

"Dot is taking this hard," Gloria said. "I'm trying to help figure out how something like this could have happened and since you were there, I thought maybe if you had a few minutes, I could talk to you to see if you can remember anything unusual about that day."

"Sure. Sure. Whatever I can do to help," Al said. "I'm just sittin' out here on my front porch drinking a cup of coffee if you want to come on over."

Gloria glanced at the clock. If she timed it right, she could visit Al and then stop by Jennifer's place to talk to her. "Sure, I'll be over there in half an hour or less...if that's not too soon."

"Not at all. I'll be here," Al answered.

Gloria headed to the bathroom. Her brain seemed to work better in the shower where there were no distractions.

After showering, she pulled on a pair of slacks and long-sleeve shirt. The morning was still a little cool but the sun was shining. It was shaping up to be a beautiful day.

She grabbed her car keys off the rack and her purse off the table.

Mally bounded around the corner of the dining room and skidded into the kitchen. She raced over to her box of stuffed animals and grabbed one off the top before meeting Gloria at the kitchen door.

"You can go with me this time," she told her. "Al's farm is about as big as this one. You'll have fun racing around his place."

The two of them hopped in the car and headed into town. Her heart sank when she passed Dot's place. It was dark.

Gloria gripped the steering wheel, a look of determination on her face. She was going to get this mystery solved, and the sooner the better.

Al's farm set back from the road a good distance. The winding path to the farm was long and narrow. Farm fields lined both sides of the drive. The fields were empty now, waiting for spring planting.

The car bumped along the path and rounded the curve.

Al's two-story white farmhouse lie straight ahead. Gloria loved Al's front porch. She liked her own porch just fine. Hers was more to the side and not big, while Al's was long and wide. It ran the entire length of the front of the house and faced west. *He must have awesome views of the sunsets and God's beautiful creation,* she thought.

Al was sitting on the porch. Gloria slowed to a stop and slid out of the car.

Al got out of his rocking chair, shoved his hands in his bib overalls and made his way down the front steps.

Al's wife, Cecelia, had died of cancer the year before. His kids tried to convince him to move in with them but he couldn't bear to part with the place. The farm had been in his family for generations, just like Gloria's husband James's farm had. Someday he hoped one of his boys would take an interest in the place. Maybe then, he would consider moving into something smaller, but for now, he was content.

He reminded Gloria of someone who was about to hop on his tractor and start tilling the fields. His eyes crinkled as he smiled at Gloria. "Good to see you Gloria."

She closed the door and made her way across the lawn to the porch. "Nice to see you, too, Al."

He waved to one of the rockers. "Have a seat," he said. "You want a cup of coffee?"

She nodded. "Sure, if you got a little extra. Black is fine."

"I'll be back in a jiffy." He disappeared inside the house as Gloria settled into the rocking chair.

Mally took off in the direction of the red silo. There was no silos on Gloria's farm and the dog was determined to check it out.

Al reappeared moments later, two coffee cups in hand. "How's Liz doin'? I heard she had you traipsing halfway across the country on some wild goose chase last week."

Gloria reached for the cup and grimaced. "She sure did. Seems she was dead set on the two of us meeting my dad's sister, Ethel. Ethel lived in Tennessee," she explained.

Al laughed. "Liz always was a firecracker," he said.

Gloria gazed at him out of the corner of her eye. Al had to be close to Liz's age.

Now that Gloria thought about it, Al asked about Liz every time she ran into him.

Liz was lonely. Al seemed lonely. Maybe she should arrange a cookout at her place with Paul and invite Liz and Al to join them...

"...and next thing I knew, the man grabbed his throat and started gagging," Al said.

Gloria had been so caught up in her matchmaking plan; she hadn't heard a single word he had said. "I'm sorry, Al. I was daydreaming. I didn't catch part of what you were saying."

Al took a sip of coffee. "No. I was just saying that Carl. You know, Carl Arnett. Carl and I were just finishing our coffee and donuts, getting ready to leave when Dot brought the chicken and dumplings out to the table next to us." He drummed his fingers on the top of his knee. "The woman with him, I guess it was his wife. She got the same thing."

He went on. "I was just getting up from the table to head to the cash register and pay when the man clutched at his throat and said something about he couldn't swallow and it felt like his throat was on fire."

Gloria remembered Dot mentioning Officer Nelson was in the restaurant that morning, too. "Was Officer Nelson still there when all this happened?"

Al nodded. "Yeah. He jumped out of his seat and ran over to try and help but I guess it was too late."

"So the man was still alive when the ambulance got there?" That was pretty much what Ray already told her.

"Yeah, but he was in rough shape. I think his throat closed shut from whatever poison was in the dumplings." He paused as he stared out at the empty field. "Ruth said something about she heard he died on the way to the hospital."

Ruth would know that, Gloria thought to herself.

"Is there anything else that sticks out in your mind as odd about the whole thing?" she asked.

"No. That was it. The police rushed us all out after they took the poor man away on the stretcher. Right after that they taped everything off."

"I appreciate your time, Al." Mally was back from her romp. She plopped down next to Gloria's chair. "We better get going."

She set the coffee cup on the small stand beside the chair. She got to her feet and started across the porch before turning back. "Thanks for the coffee."

"I was thinking about having a cookout over at my place in a week or so. Thought maybe if you had the time, you could come on over for dinner."

She went on. "I plan on inviting a few others. Margaret and Ray, Lucy and her boyfriend, Bill. Maybe my sister, Liz," she added. "And of course my boyfriend, Paul."

Al set his coffee cup on the small stand next to hers and walked to the edge of the porch. "I heard about him. Sounds like you got a keeper there."

Al's face brightened. "That is mighty nice of you Gloria," he said. "I don't get out too much other than running up to Dot's for coffee. Now I can't even do that."

She pulled her keys from her purse and started across the drive. "I'll give you call when I have a set time."

Gloria waved to Al as she pulled out of the drive. The more she thought about a cookout and inviting Al and Liz, the more she liked the idea.

What harm could a little matchmaking do?

Chapter Six

Gloria drove into town and made a last minute decision to stop at the post office, hoping that Ruth had some news. She was relieved the parking lot wasn't full of cars. There was no way Ruth and she could discuss the case if people were inside eavesdropping on their conversation.

She stepped in the front door. Ruth was leaning over the counter, talking to Beatrice. Beatrice or "Bea" as everyone in town called her, was the local hairdresser. If anyone could rival Ruth in the gossip department, it was Bea.

Ruth glanced at Gloria and Mally as they came through the door. Bea had her back to Gloria and didn't notice her standing behind her.

She caught the tail end of Bea's sentence "... and Judith said Carl told her that she heard the man's wife say something about suing Dot."

Gloria's heart skipped a beat. Dot would be devastated. *Talk of suing already?* The poor man's body wasn't even in the ground yet and his widow was ready to sue? The wife wasn't even certain who had poisoned her husband.

Bea whirled around when she heard Gloria clear her throat. "Oh. Hi Gloria."

Gloria smiled. "How you doing Bea?"

Bea straightened her back and shuffled to the side for a three-way conversation. "I'm fine. Ruth and I were just talking about the unfortunate accident over at Dot's place."

"I heard," Gloria said. "Say, does anyone know the man's name yet?"

Ruth nodded. "Yeah. Officer Joe was in here earlier. He told me they just finished the autopsy." She had a thought. "You should see if Paul can give you any info on the case," she suggested.

Gloria nodded. That was the plan. Not that that was the only reason she wanted to see Paul, although it wouldn't hurt her investigation if she could get a little insider info out of him.

Ruth went on. "His name was Mike Foley. He was from Lakeville," she said. "His wife's name is Darla." Ruth tsk-tsked. "Such a sad situation."

It was Bea's turn. "I heard. Now I don't know how true this is, but I heard that the chicken 'n dumplings were tainted with toilet bowl cleaner. Can you imagine that?" she asked.

Toilet bowl cleaner? Gloria was shocked. There was no way toilet bowl cleaner was accidentally dumped into a big pot of dumplings. Someone had to have done it on purpose.

"Did you hear the wife is talking about suing?" Ruth asked.

Gloria shook her head. "I hope not for Dot and Ray's sake..." She grabbed Mally's leash and headed for the door. This was the worst possible news she had heard all day.

She opened the door and turned back around. "I wouldn't mention it to Dot or Ray. They have enough to worry about right now."

Ruth pinched her fingers together and made a zipping motion across her mouth. "My lips are sealed."

Bea nodded. "Mine too."

Gloria closed the door. She hoped they would keep silent. The two of them didn't have a great track record for keeping secrets...

Gloria headed out of town and drove right past her own farm.

Dot's employee, Jennifer, and her husband, Tony, lived in what country folk called the boondocks.

Tony's parents ran a small sawmill on their property. They owned several acres of land

and had sectioned off a large chunk years back when Tony married Jennifer.

The two of them lived in a doublewide trailer. It had been brand new when they bought it. There was a large, open living room and it even sported a massive, stone fireplace, which Gloria loved.

Jennifer and Tony had three children. Gloria hadn't seen the kids in years. *They must be teens by now*, she thought.

The doublewide sat close to the road. Gloria noticed Jennifer's beat up four-door sedan parked in the driveway. Tony's pick-up truck was parked beside it.

Gloria pulled in behind Jennifer's car and climbed out.

Jennifer must have seen her coming. She swung the screen door open as Gloria and Mally shuffled through the grass toward the front deck.

"Hi Gloria," Jennifer said. "What brings you way out here?"

"Hey Jennifer," Gloria replied. She really liked Jennifer. The young mother hadn't been born and raised in Belhaven like her husband, Tony. She was what they jokingly referred to as a "City Slicker."

Tony met his wife long ago during a trip to Chicago. After she finished high school, she moved to Belhaven, and she and Tony married.

For years, Jennifer raised the boys while Tony worked in Green Springs at the tool and die shop. Gloria heard they cut Tony's hours back when the economy tanked.

That was another reason Jennifer was working at the restaurant. She was trying to help make ends meet until Tony could get more hours down at the shop. Thank goodness their home was on family property.

"C'mon in," Jennifer said. She patted Mally's head. "You too."

Gloria hugged Jennifer and stepped inside the house. She could hear loud, thumping music coming from somewhere in the back.

She glanced toward the kitchen. "Is Tony here?"

Jennifer shook her head. "No. He is over at the sawmill helping his dad run some boards through for a customer."

Jennifer's father-in-law, Fred, had a heart attack a few years back. He no longer worked from sun up to sun down. When Tony wasn't working at the shop, he helped his father.

Jennifer waved her hand toward the kitchen table. "You want to have a seat?"

Gloria nodded as she made her way over to the chair. "I told Dot I would come by and check on you today." She dropped her purse on the floor and Mally curled up next to her feet.

113

Jennifer pulled out a chair and plopped down. "It's just horrible, Gloria." She dropped her chin in her fist. "Dot must be devastated."

Gloria nodded. "She's taking this whole thing hard. That is why I'm here. To see if you can recall anything at all about that morning that might help track down the killer."

Jennifer glanced out the rear slider. "I got to the restaurant around eleven that day," she said. "Right around the time the breakfast crowd cleared out and before the lunch crowd started wandering in."

She went on. "I came in through the back. I remember the chicken and dumplings were already done. The big pot was sitting on the counter and the kitchen smelled heavenly." She paused. "You know how delicious Dot's dumplings are."

Gloria nodded, waiting for her to continue.

Jennifer leaned forward, her eyebrows scrunched together. "Gloria, I tasted the dumplings like I do every Wednesday morning. Not much, just a small sample. She must have just finished making them. They were piping hot."

"After I finished the dish, I put on my apron and headed to the front cuz it was starting to get busy. I was pouring coffee for your friend... uh...Andrea, when Dot stopped by the table to say she had to run down to the Quick Stop to pick up some salt."

"So it was only you and Ray running the restaurant during that time?" Gloria asked.

Jennifer nodded. "Yeah. No one was in the kitchen while Dot was gone."

"That means from the time you sampled the dumplings around eleven and the first order was served to Mike Foley and his wife, someone dumped poison in the pot," Gloria theorized.

Jennifer grabbed a pen from the center of the table and began tapping it on the tabletop. "Yeah. It had to be while Dot was down at the store."

"How long was Dot gone?" Gloria asked.

Jennifer gazed at the ceiling while she thought about it. "I would say ten minutes. Fifteen tops."

"Which meant that someone was lurking outside the back of the restaurant between 11 and 11:30 saw their opportunity to sneak inside and dump the poison in the pot and then escape out the back door without ever being seen."

They were making progress. Gloria had the timeframe narrowed down for the poisoning and determined how the killer had gained access to the restaurant.

Jennifer glanced out the rear slider again. Her husband was walking down the path towards the house. "Tony is coming," she said.

Gloria eased out of the chair and pushed it back under the table. "Is there anything else that sticks out in your mind?"

Jennifer shook her head. "The rest is a blur. I was busy waiting other tables when Dot brought the dumplings to the table."

Jennifer walked her to the door just in time for Tony to head indoors. He smiled when he saw Gloria standing in the living room.

Tony was a handsome young man. Well, young to Gloria. He had to be in his mid to late 30's by now. His sandy brown hair was parted on the side and neatly tucked behind his ears. Clean cut. That is how Gloria would describe him. He reminded her of her own two sons that she rarely saw anymore.

Her oldest son, Eddie, lived in Chicago with his wife. They didn't have children and to hear them talk, they never would.

Her middle child, Ben, lived in Houston, Texas with his wife, Kelly, and their twins, Ariel and Oliver or Ollie as they called him. The family made an effort to come back for a visit every summer but missed last year.

Gloria's grandchildren were involved in almost every kind of sport imaginable and they couldn't break away, even for a couple days.

Ben and Kelly offered to pay for Gloria's plane ticket to come visit but Gloria did not care to fly.

The last time she talked to Ben, he warned her this summer might be another no-show for them.

Gloria had already decided she would make a trip to Texas during the summer if they couldn't come home. If not, her grandkids wouldn't remember who she was.

Tony brought her back to earth when he leaned over and gave her a quick hug. "What's the special occasion?" he smiled. "No. Let me guess. You're investigating the poisoning over at Dot's place."

Gloria grinned. "Guilty as charged." She glanced at Jennifer. "I had hoped Jennifer might remember something important from the other morning."

Tony turned to his wife. He reached over and squeezed Jennifer's arm. "The whole thing shook her up. What a tragedy," he added.

Jennifer grabbed the handle on the screen door and pushed it open. "I wasn't much help. About the only thing I could remember was the time I arrived at the restaurant. I also remembered trying a small bowl of dumplings. They were delicious."

Gloria and Mally stepped onto the deck.

Tony and Jennifer followed them outside. "I wish I could remember more. Something that would help," Jennifer confessed.

Gloria hugged her. "No, you were a big help. Now I know the timeframe the pot was poisoned and that the killer came through the back kitchen door."

Jennifer walked to the railing as Gloria made her way down the steps. "You think they're going to reopen the restaurant anytime soon?"

"I hope so." Gloria shrugged. "I know you can use the money and Dot needs to stay busy and not dwell on this."

Jennifer and Tony were still standing on the deck as Gloria backed out of the driveway. She gave a small wave before pulling Annabelle onto the main road.

Her mind was in high gear. The killer knew exactly what he was doing and had the perfect timeframe to commit the crime.

Killing someone with a common household cleaning product that couldn't be traced back to a specific person was genius.

Gloria parked in her drive and made her way out to the mailbox. She pulled a small stack from the box and rifled through it as she made her way to the house.

Halfway through the stack, she spied an envelope with her name and address neatly printed on the front. She flipped the envelope over and pried it open. Inside were three sheets of paper. She unfolded the sheets. There was a small yellow sticky stuck on top. The print was too small for Gloria to read without her glasses.

Mally and she walked to the back porch. Gloria grabbed the newspaper off the steps before making her way into the kitchen. She dropped the paper on the table and reached for her reading glasses.

She read the sticky note on top of the papers first. *"Gloria, I hope this note finds you in good health. Sandy signed the waiver releasing her rights to the coins. Here are your three originals."*

The small note ended. *"Keep in touch. I'd love to hear what you all did with your coins."* The note was signed, "David Henderson."

Gloria pulled the sticky off the sheet and read the words. She didn't understand most of the mumbo-jumbo on it. She did understand the part that said Sandra McGee waived all rights and claims to the gold coins David Henderson, Gloria Rutherford, Margaret Hansen and Elizabeth Applegate found on the Henderson property.

Her hand shook as she folded the pieces of paper and stuffed them back inside the envelope. They were one step closer to being able claim a small fortune.

Chapter Seven

Gloria picked up the phone and called her sister, Liz, first.

"Hello?"

"Hey Liz. It's me. Guess what I got in the mail today?" Gloria asked. "Sandra McGee signed off on any claim to the coins."

"No way." Liz let out a shriek and dropped the phone.

Gloria pulled the phone from her ear as her sister's phone clattered to the floor.

"Sorry." Liz was back. "You still there?"

"Yep. I have three signed releases in my hot little hands," Gloria confirmed.

"That's great. I've been checking out different places where we can sell the coins," Liz said. "I also did a little research on the coins themselves. I think they're worth even more than what we originally thought."

Gloria's heart fluttered. "H-how much?" They still weren't out of the woods as far as the coins were concerned. There was still a chance the government could try to lay claim to the coins as they had to the family in Pennsylvania that the coin appraiser had mentioned.

"Millions. As in more than one," Liz said. "When do you want to get together to go over this stuff?"

"I haven't had a chance to work on my part yet," Gloria admitted. "I've been too busy trying to figure out who poisoned a customer at Dot's restaurant."

"I heard," Liz exclaimed. "That's just terrible. If anyone can figure out who did such an awful thing, it'll be you."

Gloria grinned. "I'll take that as a compliment."

"Well, it is," Liz said.

Gloria switched gears. "Hey. Before I hang up, I was wondering if you would like to come over here for a cookout next weekend."

"Just me?" Liz asked.

"No. I'm inviting Lucy and her boyfriend, Margaret and Ray, and Paul so you can finally meet him," she added. Gloria didn't mention inviting Al.

"Sure. I'll come. Can't wait to meet your beau," Liz teased.

Gloria grinned as she hung up the phone. It was the first conversation in years that she could remember where Liz and she hadn't snipped at one other.

Gloria picked up the phone again. It was time to call Margaret with the good news. No one answered the phone.

She was on her way to the fridge when she heard a light tap on the porch door.

Gloria made her way around the table. It was Margaret.

She opened the door and stepped aside. "I just left a message on your answering machine at home."

"Why?" Mally heard Margaret's voice and padded into the kitchen.

Margaret reached down and patted her head. "There's our partner-in-crime."

Gloria grabbed the papers off the kitchen table and handed one of them to Margaret.

Margaret narrowed her eyes as she attempted to read the small print. "What's this?"

"The waiver from Sandra McGee."

Margaret's head shot up. "You're kidding." She squealed before she grabbed Gloria's shoulders and danced around her. "Woo Hoo."

She folded her waiver and shoved it in her purse. "I stopped by to let you know I found some investments that look promising."

"You're way ahead of me, Margaret," Gloria warned. "I haven't had a chance to talk to a lawyer yet. The death at Dot's has been keeping me busy."

Margaret nodded. "I understand. Friends come first."

Gloria glanced at the clock above the kitchen sink. "That is another reason I called. Do you want to go over to the new restaurant in Lakeville? You know, scope it out."

"Hmm..." Margaret was only half-listening. She was staring at the front page of the local paper. "Did you see this?"

"Uh-uh. What?" Gloria leaned over Margaret's shoulder and gazed at the newspaper.

Smack dab, front and center on the first page was a photo of Dot's restaurant. The caption underneath read: "Poisoning at Local Restaurant Leads to Man's Death."

The article was a few short paragraphs. It explained how Mike Foley from nearby Lakeville was eating lunch with his wife, Darla, at Dot's when he became ill eating her lunch special, the chicken and dumplings.

The story went on to say he died on the way to the hospital. A brief mention at the end gave the funeral details.

"What are the chances someone he knew poisoned him?" Margaret asked.

"Not likely. No. I think it was someone else. Someone who was trying to harm either Dot or Ray or ruin Dot's business." She remembered the owner of Pasta Amore.

"So do you want to run over to that restaurant in Lakeville with me?" Gloria asked.

Margaret was still staring at the picture. "Yeah, yeah. Sure. When?"

"Paul is coming over for dinner tonight. How 'bout tomorrow night?"

Margaret headed for the door. "Sounds good. I think Don is going fishing with his buddies tomorrow."

Gloria watched as Margaret made her way down the steps and to her car. "Wait. What about the investments?" she yelled.

Margaret whirled around. "Oh my gosh. Can you believe I forgot why I was even here?"

Yes. Gloria could believe it. Stuff like that happened to her all the time. She could walk from the living room to the kitchen and forget why she went there.

Margaret reached into her oversize handbag and pulled out a packet. "It's a little confusing, all the types of investments. I would have Don take a look at it but even he doesn't know about the coins yet."

Margaret's husband, Don, had recently retired as vice president of a local bank.

Gloria grabbed the packet of papers and nodded. James had always taken care of their finances. She had a tidy sum in the bank, along with his pension and social security.

Gloria wasn't rich. Comfortable was a better word.

The coins weighed heavy on her mind. Sometimes money was more of a burden than a blessing. It certainly brought out the worst in certain people...

She watched Margaret drive off before heading back inside. It was time to start on dinner.

Chapter Eight

Gloria pulled some olive oil, garlic and Worcestershire sauce from the cupboard.

She cooked as she investigated her crimes - with no real follow-by-the-rule-book plans.

Gloria chopped two cloves of garlic and tossed it into the bottom of a baking dish. Next, she poured some olive oil and Worcestershire sauce in the dish.

She whisked it with a fork before dropping two ribeye steaks in the bottom. She swirled them around in the dish before flipping them over and popping them in the fridge.

It was time to head to the root cellar.

The root cellar had been a fixture on the farm for as long as Gloria could remember. It was the perfect place to store all her vegetables. The farm's root cellar was partially below ground and there were several steps leading down to it.

She grabbed a flashlight by the door before heading outdoors in search of some potatoes. There were still a bunch left over from the previous season's garden.

Gloria made her way down the steps to the wooden red doors. She opened the doors, clicked on the flashlight and stepped inside. A cool dampness hung in the air.

She shivered as she made her way to the back of the cellar.

There was a small stockpile of potatoes, a few onions, some carrots and a couple heads of cabbage.

Gloria grabbed two nice-sized potatoes and an onion.

Mally had followed her to the cellar and sniffed around the storage bins. "Sorry girl. I don't have any corn."

Mally dropped her head and followed Gloria up the cement steps. Corn on the cob was her favorite.

"Don't worry. I plan on growing at least three rows of yellow corn this summer just for you," she promised.

The day had warmed nicely, thanks to the bright sunshine. Gloria was thankful for the lovely weather.

There was nothing worse than trying to grill steaks in the cold - or worse yet - rain.

Back inside, she scrubbed the potatoes and set them aside.

She glanced at Mally and Puddles, who had wandered into the kitchen in search of a snack. "I know, I know. We're all hungry."

She fed them both before pulling a bowl of vegetable soup from the freezer. While she waited for the soup to thaw in the microwave, she picked up the newspaper and glanced at the article again.

She prayed Dot hadn't seen it, but chances of that were slim.

Gloria opened the paper and studied the inside. Three pages in, her eyes zeroed in on a restaurant review. She picked up her glasses and started to read:

"Pasta Amore Makes Me Want Some Moray" the headline read. It was a five-star review of the new restaurant. According to the food critic, who had ordered the sampler platter...baked lasagna, chicken piccata and five-cheese ziti, the food was fabulous.

The critic ranted and raved about the creamy pasta, fresh spices and crusty, garlic bread. The author even gushed over the salad, how the dressing had the perfect amount of tang. The critic also pointed out how the croutons were fresh and made from scratch.

Gloria finished reading the review and then studied the photo of the food critic. It was a young woman with long dark hair. *Amy Martola.*

She doesn't look old enough to be an experienced food critic, Gloria decided. When Margaret and I eat there tomorrow night, I'm going to try that sampler plate myself, she vowed.

She tugged the grocery store insert from the paper and started a short grocery list as she ate her soup.

Her fridge was almost empty. Even though she didn't mind going to the store, it wasn't at the top of her list of favorite things to do.

Gloria carried her dishes to the sink when the phone started to ring.

It was her daughter, Jill. "Hi Mom. How was the trip to Tennessee?"

Gloria propped the phone on her shoulder and picked up the dishrag and bowl. "It was fine.

Margaret and I had a very nice time. Your Aunt Liz was a bit of a stinker but straightened up toward the end," she added.

Jill chuckled. Her Aunt Liz was a bit of a handful, but in a good way. "The boys and I thought we would make a trip to the flea market on Thursday. You want to go with us?" she asked.

Gloria didn't get to spend a lot of time with Jill and the boys these days. It would be nice to see them. "Yes, of course. What time?"

"How does nine sound? We can eat breakfast at Dot's and then walk to the flea market," Jill said.

Oh no. Jill didn't know about Dot's. "You don't get the local newspaper, do you?" Gloria asked.

"No. Why?" Jill replied.

"Because Dot's restaurant is closed right now. Someone died after eating her chicken and dumplings last Wednesday."

Jill sucked in her breath. "You're kidding."

"I wish I was. The place is shut down until the health department and police department give them the all clear to open back up," Gloria explained.

Tears filled Jill's eyes. Her heart went out to poor Dot, who was like a second mother to her. "Poor Dot."

"I'm trying to figure out what happened and clear Dot's and Ray's good name," Gloria said.

"If anyone can figure out what happened, it's you," Jill said confidently.

Gloria smiled. That was the second compliment she'd received that day on her sleuthing abilities.

The smile faded when she remembered one of her favorite sayings, *"Pride Goeth Before a Fall."*

Jill yelled into the phone. "Tyler, put that down. Listen, I gotta go. Tyler is spraying the dog with air freshener."

"Okay. See you next week," Gloria quickly replied. Jill was already gone.

Gloria shook her head and offered up a small prayer for Jill and extra patience with her grandsons.

Gloria glanced at the clock. It was time to start on her secret weapon. Dessert.

The way to a man's heart was through his stomach. She remembered him mentioning that he loved coconut. With that in mind, she knew what to make. Creamy coconut cake.

She plugged in her portable radio and turned it to a Christian radio station.

Next, Gloria gathered the ingredients and placed them on the counter.

The afternoon flew by as she busied herself with the special dinner.

Her mind wandered to Liz and Al as she worked. Maybe the two of them would hit it off. Al seemed laid back while Liz could be high maintenance. One never could tell. He might be the perfect balance to her personality.

Gloria shrugged. It was worth a shot. If nothing else, maybe they could be friends...

The ringing phone pulled her from deep thought. She wiped her hands on her daisy print apron. "Hello?"

"Hello Gloria." Gloria's face grew warm. It was Paul. She pulled the phone closer. "Don't tell me you're calling to cancel dinner," she groaned.

"No. Not at all," he reassured her. "I'm getting off a little early and thought I'd head over to your place now..." he trailed off.

Everything was almost ready to go. All she had to do was freshen up. "Sure. Come on over."

After they hung up, she made a beeline for the bathroom. He was only half an hour ahead of schedule so it wasn't a big deal.

Gloria freshened her make-up and checked her outfit one last time. She decided on a pair of dark blue capris and baby blue silk blouse.

On her feet were a pair of black flats. She popped a pair of pearl earrings in her ears and spritzed some of her favorite perfume on before she wandered back into the kitchen.

She got there just in time to see his squad car pull into the drive. Her heart sank. The squad car meant just one thing. *He has to work early tomorrow morning*, she thought.

She swung the door open and stepped out onto the porch. Her pulse raced as she watched his tall, broad-shouldered figure emerge from the driver's seat.

He reached back inside the car and pulled a hanging basket of flowers from the passenger seat.

"Flowers again?" she said.

"Of course," he replied. "These are for the porch."

He leaned close and sniffed the air. "You smell pretty."

Gloria smiled brightly. "Thanks." She turned and waved him up the steps. "C'mon inside."

She hung the colorful arrangement from a hook on the porch before they headed indoors.

Gloria pulled a pitcher of lemonade from the fridge, along with the steaks still marinating in the dish. He grabbed the steaks while she poured the lemonade.

"We can sit out on the porch while these are grilling," she suggested.

She settled in the rocker and watched as he fired up the grill.

The sun began to set in the sky. For a moment, it reminded Gloria of several months earlier when she sat in the exact same rocker and faced the sunset. Her life was much different back then than it was now.

She had been alone...and lonely. As she reflected back on it, it was a season in her life where she felt as if she had no purpose. She remembered praying to God to help her become useful again.

It wasn't long after that Daniel Malone's body was found in the woods behind the old elementary school.

Gloria dove head first into detective-mode, something that had always intrigued her. Things began to change after that. She helped solve Daniel Malone's murder – Andrea's husband.

She glanced at Paul out of the corner of her eye. That was how she had met Paul.

He had been the detective handling the Malone murder case. Gloria visited the police station more than once to turn in clues she uncovered.

She remembered that day, too. How nervous she had been sitting across from him in his office.

Gloria wondered now if she had been nervous because she'd never been inside a police station before or perhaps maybe, just maybe, she was the teensiest bit attracted to him. You know what they say – love at first sight.

Maybe her heart knew something that hadn't registered in her head yet. Either way, she was thankful God brought her to the station that day.

Paul reached over and grabbed Gloria's hand. "You're a million miles away..."

She smiled. "Just remembering how we met."

Paul slid into the rocker next to her. "Did you think I was cute back then?" he teased.

Gloria blushed. "I guess I did."

They chatted easily about living on the farm and how peaceful it was.

Paul pulled the steaks from the grill and set them on the plate next to it. Gloria held the door as he made his way inside. She glanced behind her.

The sunset was spectacular. Her eyes settled on the small bistro table in the corner. "What if I throw a tablecloth on the porch table and we eat out here?" she suggested.

His eyebrows raised. "Hmm. That sounds romantic..."

"You're right." She opened a kitchen drawer and grabbed the first tablecloth she found. She unfolded it and inspected the front, which was dotted with bowls of fruit and edged in lime green gingham print.

Romantic, it was not, but at least it was something. She shoved the drawer closed and made her way back to the porch. She slid the table away from the railing before draping the plastic cloth over the top.

Gloria picked up an old rag and wiped the metal chairs before heading back inside. Paul pulled the garlic bread from the oven while Gloria grabbed butter and sour cream from the fridge and carried them outside.

After the table was set, Paul followed behind with the steaks.

She scooted in while he grabbed the second chair and slid it close to hers. The angle of the chairs gave them a front row view of the setting sun.

He refilled their lemonade glasses and handed her one. "Here's to a spectacular view of God's masterpiece and the beautiful woman beside me."

Gloria sipped the tart concoction, and studied him over the rim of her glass. He must have really missed her while she was gone.

Gloria sliced her baked potato down the center, dumped a thick wedge of butter and glob of sour cream in the middle before she squeezed the potato back together. She cut a generous piece of steak and set it on a napkin nearby.

"Midnight snack?" Paul joked.

Gloria smiled. "No. A treat for Mally and Puddles."

He nodded before popping a piece of steak in his mouth. The tender, juicy slice was grilled to perfection. He savored the bite before he swallowed. "This is the best steak I've ever tasted," he mumbled in between bites.

"You're biased," Gloria argued.

Paul shrugged. "Perhaps." He pointed his knife at the meat. "This steak almost melts in my mouth."

Gloria took her first bite. She had to agree. It was delicious. It wasn't overcooked, just a tad past medium, which was perfect. "Mmmm. You're right. It is delicious."

She squeezed her potato open and flattened it with her fork before spreading the butter and sour cream around. After a couple quick shakes of salt and pepper, it was time to taste.

She scooped a pile on her fork and popped it in her mouth. Even after being in the root cellar all winter, the potato tasted as if she had just dug it from the garden.

Paul lifted a forkful of potato to his mouth. "Did you grow this yourself?" he asked.

Gloria nodded. "Last year."

He took another bite. "Wow. You would never know."

Gloria thought now would be the perfect opportunity to ask him about the poisoning at Dot's restaurant.

"How's the Mike Foley investigation going?"

Paul laid his fork on the plate. He studied Gloria's face for a moment. "You're still working on this one..."

Gloria stabbed at the pile of green beans. She pulled the fork to her mouth and nibbled on the end. "Of course. Dot is beside herself. I'm going to do whatever I can to help."

Paul ran his finger along the rim of his glass. "You know I can't tell you much."

She nodded. "I know, but if I guess can you nod your head?"

"Hmm...Depends on the question."

"Is it true the victim was poisoned by toilet bowl cleaner?" she asked.

He drummed his fingers on the plastic tablecloth. "Yeah. It was your everyday buy-it-in-any-grocery-store toilet bowl cleaner."

It was his turn to ask. "Do you have any suspects yet?"

"Mmhmm."

"Let me guess," he replied. "It's not Dot."

"Nope," Gloria agreed. "Not even close."

"Are you going to tell me or am I going to have to use my special interrogation tactics on you?" he threatened.

Her eyes twinkled and she grinned. "That sounds interesting."

She shook her head. "No, I don't mind sharing. I actually have a few." She told him about Judith Arnett, who tried to steal from Dot just before the poisoning.

She brought up the owner of Pasta Amore.

"That doesn't make him a suspect," Paul pointed out.

"No, but it doesn't NOT make him a suspect. I just think it was too convenient that he opened his new restaurant at almost the exact same time Dot's customer was poisoned."

"Anyone else?" he asked.

"Not yet," she admitted. "But I'm still interviewing witnesses."

They finished their meal as the sun dropped below the horizon. The clouds dotting the sky reminded Gloria of a painting.

She wondered if heaven had the same view. There were hues of pink and blue with tinges of orange filling the sky. "So pretty," she murmured.

Paul piled the plates on top of each other. He stopped for a moment to admire the view. "Great idea, Gloria. We need to do this more often," he said.

They cleared the table. Gloria wiped the plastic tablecloth dry and folded it up. She hadn't used the thing in years but tonight, it found a purpose again.

Just like me, she thought. *Never too old to have a purpose.*

They finished dinner with a cup of freshly brewed coffee and a slice of coconut cake with a scoop of vanilla bean ice cream on the side. The layered treat was confectionary perfection.

Paul finished his piece before Gloria was halfway done with hers. She caught him eyeing the dessert and pushed the dessert toward him. "Here, have another piece," she urged.

He reached for the plate and then paused. "Are you sure?"

"Yes, of course. I made it for you," she answered. He sliced another piece and eased it onto his plate.

Gloria watched him take a bite. "I was thinking about having a cookout and inviting a few friends and family over," she said.

"You haven't met Liz yet and she has been hinting. Well...not really a hint. She came right out and asked when she was going to meet you."

Paul grinned. He couldn't wait to meet the infamous Liz. "Who else?"

She ticked off her mental list. "Lucy and her boyfriend, Bill. Dot and Ray. Margaret and Don. Ruth. I think you met her once."

Paul nodded.

"Liz, of course. And Al Dickerson," she finished. "Al is a widower."

Paul raised his eyebrows. "Matchmaking?" he guessed.

Gloria scraped the last bit of creamy coconut off her dessert plate and ate it. "I wouldn't necessarily call it matchmaking. Just inviting a lonely widower from town over for a get-together."

Paul pushed his chair back and carried his plate to the sink.

Gloria followed behind and dropped hers on top. "Although, if they ended up liking each other, what's the harm in that?"

Paul spun around to face Gloria. He reached out, wrapped his arms around her waist and pulled her close. "What are you going to do if both Ruth *and* Liz take a liking to this Al Dickerson?"

Gloria's brows furrowed. She hadn't thought about that. Maybe she should find another eligible bachelor in town and invite him....even up the guest list.

Paul released his hold and took a step back. He glanced up at the wall clock. It was getting late. "I better go. I'm working the early shift tomorrow."

Paul yawned and stretched his arms high above his head. "Four-thirty creeps up on me fast."

Gloria grabbed a foam plate from the cupboard and slid a large piece of cake onto the plate. She covered the rest with plastic wrap. "For breakfast tomorrow," she joked.

He patted his stomach. "You sure know the way to a man's heart."

A lump formed in Gloria throat. She was sad to see him go. The evening had gone by much too fast.

Mally and Gloria followed him out to his car. She waited for him to slide into the driver's seat before handing the cake through the open window. "If I plan a cookout on Saturday, can you make it?"

"I wouldn't miss this for the world." He started the car. "I hope it doesn't backfire on you."

Gloria didn't think it would. After all, it was just a cookout.

She watched as his car pulled out of the driveway before Mally and she made their way back inside.

Chapter Nine

Sunday morning rolled around and for the first time in her life that Gloria could remember, she overslept on a Sunday.

It was her favorite day of the week and she never missed church - unless she was sick, or out of town as she had been the previous week when Margaret and she were trying to track down Liz.

She threw back the covers and scrambled from the bed. There was no time to make it.

She rushed to the kitchen and started a pot of coffee before heading to the shower. After a quick scrub down, she wiggled into her favorite pink skirt and slipped on the matching jacket.

Spring was here and the outfit needed a touch more color.

Gloria grabbed a bright yellow scarf – her favorite color – from the scarf rack and quickly tied it around her neck.

She slid into her pink heels and hurried to the kitchen.

Mally was waiting for her at the door. She thumped her tail on the linoleum and whined. "I know. You need to go out. Just a sec."

She grabbed a coffee cup from the cupboard and poured half a cup, knowing she wouldn't have time to drink a whole one.

Gloria followed Mally out the door and stood there enjoying the cool morning air as she watched the dog romp around the garden.

One more week and it would be time to start planting. "You better enjoy tearing that up while you can. Pretty soon, it'll be off limits until fall," she warned.

Mally stopped for a second. She tilted her head to the side as she considered Gloria's words. She let out a small "woof" before following Gloria back into the house.

Mally settled into her doggie bed while Gloria grabbed her car keys and purse. The dog knew it was Sunday and she wasn't allowed to go to church. "I'll be back before you know it," Gloria promised.

Mally thumped her tail as Gloria closed the door behind her and locked it.

Gloria pulled Annabelle into the church parking lot. The lot was full and she was late. Later than normal.

She found an open spot in the back. Andrea pulled in right behind her and into the empty spot beside Gloria.

Andrea slid out of her sleek Mercedes and met Gloria near the trunk of the car. "I thought I was late," she said.

The girls headed to the front door. Justin was standing just inside. He handed a church bulletin to Gloria. "Good morning Mrs. Rutherford."

He turned to Andrea; a bright smile lit his whole face. "Good morning Andrea."

Andrea's cheeks turned a tad pink. "Hi Justin," she said.

There was no time to chat. Others were coming in behind them so they moved along.

"Are you two dating?" Gloria didn't want to pry but couldn't help herself.

"He asked me to dinner next week," Andrea whispered back.

"And?" Gloria prompted.

"Well..." She stopped. She liked Justin but she didn't "like-like" him, if that made any sense.

"Do what makes you happy, dear," Gloria advised. "Don't be surprised if you become public enemy number one with all the other young ladies in this town. They have been chasing poor Justin for years without any luck."

Andrea bit her lower lip and her eyebrows drew together. "You think so? I don't need to make any more enemies than I already have," she fretted.

Gloria patted her arm. "Don't worry. We will nip that in the bud if it ever happens," she promised.

The girls started down the center aisle just as Slick Steve (as Gloria secretly nicknamed him) was coming from the other direction.

He paused when he got close. "Good morning ladies. You look lovely today."

Steve Colby had moved to their small town of Belhaven almost a year ago. During that time, he dated several of the single and widowed women in town. He had a reputation for taking them out a few times and then fading away. To put it bluntly, he was leaving a trail of broken hearts.

Gloria was ready to give him her standard, no-nonsense "thank you" when she had a sudden change of heart. "Nice to see you Steve."

Steve's eyebrows shot up at the unexpected warmth in Gloria's voice. She was not normally warm and fuzzy. At least not to him.

She went on. "I'm planning a cookout next weekend - next Saturday night. I know you're still kind of new in town and thought it might be nice to have you over - along with a few other people from Belhaven."

"I-I uh. Yeah. Thanks Gloria. I would like that," he stammered.

"Good. Give me your number and I'll give you a call later this week to confirm the time."

After they walked away, Andrea whispered. "I thought you didn't like him."

"Everyone deserves a second chance." Perhaps Gloria had been too hard on him. After all, she only got one side of the story...the jilted women's side. "Besides, I have a logical explanation for inviting him."

Gloria spied Dot sitting on an end pew. She eased onto the bench next to her as Andrea settled in on the other side.

Gloria reached over and squeezed Dot's hand. "I'm so glad you're here."

Dot nodded. "I almost didn't come but changed my mind at the last minute."

Gloria studied her friend out of the corner of her eye. She looked much better today. "Margaret and I are having dinner at Pasta Amore tonight to – you know." She gave her a hard stare. "You want to come?"

Dot stared blankly and then it dawned on her. "Yes. Yes, I think I would," she decided.

Gloria turned to Andrea. "How 'bout you, Andrea? You want to have dinner at Pasta Amore with us?"

Andrea shrugged. "Sure. As long as I won't be in the way of your investigation."

"No. Not at all," Gloria reassured her young friend. The more she thought about it, the more she liked the idea. After all, four heads were better than one.

Maybe the others would notice something Gloria might otherwise miss.

The service started. "We'll talk about it after church," Gloria whispered.

Pastor Nate's sermon was thought provoking. The message was about confusing your season in life with your destiny. How God allows trials in our lives to strengthen our faith. The key verse was fitting:

For You, O God, tested us; You refined us like silver. Psalms 66:10-12 NIV.

Gloria glanced over at Dot. Her heart lurched as she saw the bright glimmer of tears that threatened to spill down her cheeks.

After the service ended, the girls congregated in the grassy area off to the side.

Margaret was the first to speak. "I'm glad you made it to church this morning, Dot. We've been worried about you."

Ruth chimed in. "We're here for you, Dot. You and Ray," she added.

Lucy linked arms with Dot. "We're in this together," she vowed.

Dot's eyes filled with tears again. "I don't deserve such good friends," she whispered.

Andrea's eyes wandered from one to the other. "You all are so blessed to have each other."

"Hey, you're part of this group now. We're blessed to have you, too." Lucy pointed out.

Gloria looked up. Justin was on his way over. "I have a couple things to say before I forget." She held up an index finger. "First.

Margaret, Dot, Andrea and I are heading over to Pasta Amore in Lakeville for dinner tonight."

She turned to Ruth. "You still want to go?"

Ruth nodded. "Sure, what time?"

Lucy shook her head. "I'm out. Bill and his kids are coming over for barbecue."

"Which reminds me of my second thing." Gloria raised a second finger. "I'm having a cookout at my house next Saturday at six and you are all invited. Including spouses." She turned to Lucy. "And boyfriends."

"Sounds like fun," Lucy chimed in. "Someone else cooking other than me."

Gloria lifted a third finger. "Last but not least, who is visiting the shut-ins today?"

Some weeks all the girls made the rounds together. Other times, only one or two could make it. Lucy and Ruth raised their hands.

"Okay, meet me in front of Dot's in an hour," she ordered. "For the rest going to Pasta Amore, we can meet at Ruth's place and since she has a van, we can all ride together."

They agreed to meet up at five before the group disbanded.

Gloria decided the plan for dinner was perfect. The girls could talk to Andrea to see if she remembered anything from the morning of the unfortunate incident at Dot's Restaurant. Maybe Dot could remember something else.

Back at the farm, she fixed a tuna fish sandwich and carried that and a bag of chips onto the porch.

She worked on her Saturday night cookout menu as she watched Mally chase a pair of squirrels around the yard. "Don't go near the road," Gloria yelled.

Mally stopped short. She knew she was getting too close to the street. She dropped her head and slunk her way back to the porch.

Gloria tore a piece of her sandwich off and offered it to Mally. She patted her head. "I didn't mean to yell. You just got too close and I was worried," she explained.

Gloria started on a second list. This one was more pressing. She needed to put together a list of questions to ask the girls about that fateful day. She jotted down some thoughts and set the paper aside when she heard a loud "meow."

Puddles was not happy he had been left inside while Gloria and Mally were out on the porch enjoying the nice weather.

Gloria opened the door and Puddles stalked past. He sniffed around the edge of the railing. For a moment, he looked as if he was headed down the steps. Puddles did an abrupt about face and leapt onto Gloria's lap instead.

Gloria stroked Puddles' fluffy back and then leaned her head against the rocker. She closed her eyes for just a minute and drifted off. She awoke to Mally who was nudging her leg. Her eyes flew open. She had fallen asleep.

She carried Puddles inside the house. Mally followed behind. Her eyes darted to the clock. She had fallen asleep for over half an hour.

It was time to visit the shut-ins. She tore through the house to get ready and in ten minutes flat was back out the door and in the car.

By the time she got back home from the visits, she had to turn right around and head over to Ruth's place.

Gloria was the last to pull in the drive. Margaret, Dot and Andrea were already there.

"We were beginning to think you changed your mind," Ruth said.

"Just running a little late, that's all." She made a mental note not to overbook her days. It was wearing her out.

The girls spent the time in the van discussing Dot's case.

Gloria went over her list of suspects and why.

"Is it possible Judith was the one who snuck in the back door?" Ruth wondered.

Gloria turned to Andrea. "Do you know who we're talking about?"

Andrea shook her head. "I know that I have heard her name but can't say if I've ever seen her before."

Ruth pulled the van into an empty spot in front of Pasta Amore. She grabbed the door handle.

Gloria reached over and stopped her. "Wait."

Margaret groaned. "Oh no. Not another stakeout."

Gloria shook her head. "No. At least not an official one. I would like to sit here for a few minutes if you don't mind."

Dot clasped her hands in her lap. "If Gloria says wait – we wait."

The restaurant had just opened their doors for dinner. The girls studied the customers as they wandered inside.

Gloria was ready to give up and head in herself when she noticed a lone woman strolling down the sidewalk. She looked familiar. "I've seen her before."

Margaret nodded. "Me too."

"In the restaurant?" Dot wondered.

It was right on the edge of Gloria's head. "No..."

Gloria snapped her fingers. "I've got it. She is the food critic." She whacked the side of Margaret's arm. "I saw her picture in the newspaper. She wrote a review on this restaurant. A glowing review," she added.

Margaret's eyes widened. "You're right. I saw the same article."

"If she just reviewed the restaurant the other day, what is she doing back here so soon? Surely not another review..." Ruth said.

Gloria grabbed the door handle. "Good question. Time to find out."

The girls climbed out of the van and made their way inside.

Gloria's eyes darted around the room in search of the dark-haired woman. "What was her name?" she whispered to Margaret.

"Amy something..."

Dot grabbed Andrea's arm. "She's over there."

They didn't want to chance having the hostess seat them somewhere else so they hurried over to the open table next to where the young woman sat.

Gloria picked the chair directly behind Amy.

Dot plopped down in a chair across from her so she could watch her. More like shoot daggers at the side of her head. "Dot."

Dot's head snapped toward Margaret. "What?"

"You're glaring," she pointed out.

"Okay, Okay. I'll stop."

The waitress appeared at their table with a tray of ice waters and menus. "Welcome to Pasta Amore," she said. "Have you dined with us before?"

"Yes."

"No."

"Some of us have and some of us haven't," Gloria explained.

"Well, we're happy you're here. Our special today is spaghetti and meatballs."

Gloria's eyes darted to Dot. One of Dot's dinner specials was spaghetti and meatballs.

Dot's face turned beet red and she clenched her fist.

Gloria stuck her head behind the menu and leaned in Dot's direction. "Remember, it's an Italian restaurant," she mumbled under her breath.

The waitress jotted their orders on her notepad and headed to the kitchen. She passed a man coming from the opposite direction. He was the same man that Dot and Gloria met in the back alley the other day.

He strode across the dining room and stopped at the table behind theirs.

"Hello Amy," the man said.

"Hi Uncle Joe," she replied.

"Uncle Joe." Gloria mouthed the words. The food critic was related to this man? *No wonder he got such a raving restaurant review.*

They talked for several minutes before he headed back to the kitchen.

The waitress returned with their drinks. "The man that just walked out here... Is he the owner of Pasta Amore?" Gloria asked.

The woman set an iced tea in front of Gloria. "Yes, that's the owner. Joe Toscani."

Bingo. Gloria had a name now. She repeated the name to herself three times. It was a trick she used to memorize important information.

There was no need to worry about that. Ruth was scribbling furiously on her drink napkin. She shoved the napkin in her purse and winked at Gloria.

Dinner arrived a short time later. Gloria had to admit the food was good.

"The food is good," Dot announced.

"Not as good as yours," Andrea argued.

The others agreed with Andrea.

Dot swirled the spaghetti around her fork. "You're just trying to make me feel better."

The owner didn't make a second appearance and the food critic behind them ate alone so the eavesdropping ended.

The girls divvied up the bill and paid before making their way back to the van.

The girls buckled in as Ruth backed out of the spot. "We got some valuable information."

Gloria agreed. "We know the owner's name."

"Yep, and we know one more thing," Andrea announced.

"What is that?" Margaret wondered aloud.

"Joe Toscani was in your restaurant the morning of the poisoning. I remember seeing him."

Chapter Ten

The color drained from Dot's face. "You're kidding?"

Andrea shook her head. "No. I'm positive he was in Dot's restaurant eating breakfast. The reason I remember," she explained, "was because he was complaining rather loudly about how his eggs were overcooked."

She went on. "Jennifer took care of it. She tried to get him to wait while she brought out a new order but the man didn't want to wait. The more she tried to help, the more irate he became."

"It was almost as if he was trying to make a scene," Andrea added. "He left not long afterward. Stormed out the door."

"That was before the man was poisoned?" Ruth asked.

Andrea nodded. "Yeah. Wasn't long after that Dot came back and served the dumplings to the couple."

Gloria spoke her thoughts. "He had motive and he had opportunity." She couldn't wait to get home and log onto her computer to find out what was up with the guy.

The house was dark when Gloria pulled into the driveway. She stuck her leftovers from dinner in the fridge before letting Mally out.

She followed her out onto the porch. The night air was cool and a light breeze made it even chillier. Gloria rubbed her upper arms to ward off the chill.

Gloria studied the outline of her big red barn as she thought about the man that had been hiding out in there a few months back.

"C'mon, girl. Time to go in."

She fed Mally and Puddles while she waited for her computer to boot up. Even if this

Joe was a killer, how could she ever prove it? So far, no one had seen anything or anyone suspicious that day.

Gloria settled into the desk chair and logged into her email before starting her search. Her fingers fumbled clumsily on the keys. It took three tries to type in the correct spelling. "*Joseph Toscani, Chicago, Illinois.*"

She held her breath as the computer searched. It was worth the wait. The first thing that popped up on her screen indicated he was the owner of Amici Trattoria. She clicked on the link.

The news article was three months old. *Joseph Toscani, the owner of Amici Trattoria, is being investigated by the Chicago Police Department in the suspicious death of his business partner, Giuseppe Serafino.*

The two men were co-owners of the Amici Trattoria. Prior to Mr. Serafino's death, an undercover investigation into their business had been ongoing for several months.

Mr. Serafino's body was found under a bridge near the Chicago River on the morning of January 1st. An autopsy revealed Mr. Serafino was strangled to death. Police believe he was killed prior to his body being placed near the river.

Mr. Serafino's partner, Joseph Toscani, is the prime suspect. Police have uncovered mob connections to both Mr. Serafino and Mr. Toscani.

The article ended by saying so far Joseph Toscani had not been charged with the murder.

Gloria leaned in to have a closer look at Toscani's photo. The girls had seen the same man earlier in the restaurant.

Joseph Toscani was a killer. But would he risk killing again, just to eliminate his competition in a town as small as Lakeville?

Gloria thought of something else. *Was his niece, Amy Martola, in on it?*

She thought about Judith, who had been seen around town that morning, too. Perhaps she tried to poison Dot.

If only there was some way she could get her hands on the poison.

Gloria chewed her lower lip. Today was Sunday. The incident happened four days earlier.

Gloria shoved back the chair and made a beeline for the phone in the kitchen.

"Hello?" Dot answered on the first ring.

"Hey Dot. It's me – Gloria."

"Oh. Hi Gloria. What's up?"

"I was just wondering...what day is trash pick-up at the restaurant?" Gloria asked.

"Monday," Dot said. "Early Monday morning," she added.

Gloria glanced out the window. It was already dark out - but she needed to search the trash before the trash collectors picked it up the next morning.

"Why?" Dot asked.

"I want to take a look inside the garbage cans out back," Gloria confessed.

"Y-you think there might be some kind of evidence inside?" Dot asked.

"It's worth a shot," Gloria replied. "Look, if it's okay with you, I'm going to run down to the restaurant."

She glanced at Mally sprawled out in her doggy bed. "I'll take Mally with me."

"Sure Gloria," Dot agreed. "You want me to meet you down there?"

"That's up to you," she answered. "All I know is I need to sift through the cans before they get picked up."

Dot tightened her grip on the phone. "I can help. I'll meet you there in ten minutes."

Gloria grabbed her purse from the chair and her car keys from the hook. "C'mon Mally." She started out the door and then turned back.

Gloria would almost bet that the trash smelled to high heaven.

She grabbed a couple garbage bags and pair of latex kitchen gloves from underneath the sink before the two of them hopped in Annabelle and headed to town.

Main Street was empty, except for cars in front of Kip's Bar & Grill. The red neon sign flashed brightly above the front door. Kip's wasn't really a "grill." Just a bar.

The food menu was limited to the kind of stuff you would find in a convenience store - hot dogs on a rotisserie, pre-packed hamburgers and nuked-to-order frozen pizzas.

Gloria turned right and headed down the alley. She pulled into the small grassy lot behind the restaurant.

Dot's van was already there. Mally and she slid out of the car.

Dot met her by the driver's side door. "Why didn't I think of this?" she asked.

"I didn't, either, Dot. Not until tonight." Gloria replied. "Better late than never."

Dot opened her purse and pulled out a flashlight. "I figured we would want to keep a low profile."

Gloria nodded. "You're getting the hang of this sleuthing thing." She turned her own flashlight on. "Especially since the killer is still on the loose."

Dot, Mally and Gloria hugged the edge of the building and made their way to the back door.

"You really should put up some kind of light back here," Gloria commented.

"I know, I know. Ray and I keep telling each other that."

Gloria flashed her light back and forth across the rear of the restaurant's drab gray exterior. "Where's the trash?"

Dot pointed. "Off to the side."

Gloria tiptoed to the side of the building and shined her light between the restaurant and the building beside it.

There were two trashcans. One was a large, plastic green bin on wheels and the other a smaller, round metal bin. "Which is which?" she whispered behind her.

"The green one is regular trash and the metal one is recyclables," Dot told her.

"Here, hold this." Gloria handed her flashlight to Dot and grabbed the plastic bin with

185

the wheels. She wheeled it to the back of the building and onto the cement pad outside the kitchen door.

"Let's grab the other one," Gloria said.

The flashlight bobbed brightly as the girls made their way around the side of the building.

Gloria grabbed both handles and tried lifting it. The metal container wouldn't budge. "This one is too heavy."

Dot squeezed past Gloria as she made her way around the other side of the metal can.

She tucked the flashlight in her front pocket and grabbed the side handle with both hands.

Gloria grabbed the other side and the girls half-carried, half-dragged the can down the narrow space and onto the cement pad.

They set it next to the other can.

Dot lifted the lid on the green bin first. Gloria gagged as the smell of rotting vegetables and putrid fish exploded in the night air. She turned her head to escape the smell and plugged her nose. "That is disgusting," she wheezed.

It was apparent that Dot was accustomed to bad smells. "It's not that bad."

Gloria waved a hand across her face before she pulled the flashlight from her pocket and pointed the light into the open can.

Dot wrinkled her nose. "I'm not so sure about digging through this."

Gloria took a step back. "Yuck. Me either." She shined her flashlight on the metal can. "Let's try this one instead."

She popped the top off the can and laid it on the ground beside her. At first glance, all Gloria saw were soda cans, flattened cardboard boxes and empty plastic milk cartons. "Wow. You're a good recycler," Gloria complimented.

Dot smiled. "Thanks. I do try. No sense throwing recycle material in landfills and polluting the earth."

Gloria pulled a rubber glove from her purse and slipped it on. She held onto the flashlight with her other hand as she pushed the contents around. "Grab the garbage bag from my purse and we will start sorting through this stuff."

The words were no more out of her mouth when she laid eyes on something blue with a red plastic tip. Gloria's heart skipped a beat. "Wait. I think we found something."

Her eyes widened as she glanced over at Dot. "Do you see that?"

Dot shook her head. "No."

Gloria waved a gloved hand. "Over here."

Dot scooted over to where Gloria was standing. "Right there."

Dot craned her neck, leaned forward and gasped.

Chapter Eleven

Gloria stuck her gloved hand inside the trashcan and plucked out an empty bottle of toilet bowl cleaner. "Does this look familiar?"

Dot shook her head. "No. We don't use that kind." She reached out to touch the bottle.

"Don't touch it," Gloria shrieked. "This is evidence and we don't want your fingerprints on it."

Dot snatched her hand back. "You're right."

"Open the trash bag and I'll put it inside," Gloria said.

Dot obediently opened the bag while Gloria dropped the cleaner inside and tied the bag shut. "I need to get this over to the police department so they can test for fingerprints."

Dot exhaled the breath she'd been holding. "You think the killer was stupid enough to leave the evidence in my trash can?"

Gloria shook her head. "Dumber things have happened."

The girls emptied the recycle can on the cement floor and sifted through the rest of the contents. Nothing else appeared to be a clue.

They dumped the trash back inside and pulled that and the other container to the edge of the alley for the morning pick up.

Gloria peeled off the plastic gloves and dropped them on top. "I'm going to run this by the station before I head home," she said.

Dot nodded. "I've been praying, Gloria. I hope this is the break in the case we've been searching for."

Gloria opened the passenger's side door and set the trash bag on the seat. "Me too. I'll let you know what I find out."

Dot's voice quivered. "Thanks for being such a good friend, Gloria."

Tears stung the back of Gloria's eyes. "I know you would do the same for me, Dot."

Without saying another word, Gloria and Mally climbed into the car. Instead of turning toward home, they headed in the direction of Montbay Sheriff's office – and Paul.

***

Gloria pulled up in front of the station and turned the car off. She grabbed the trash bag before opening the door.

Mally scrambled across the seat. "Sorry, girl. You can't go with me. I'll be right back," she promised.

It didn't stop Mally from giving her "that look" but there wasn't much Gloria could do.

She hurried across the street, up the stairs and in the front entrance. A young, shorthaired brunette was behind the counter. Her head popped up when Gloria walked through the door. She smiled. "Can I help you?"

Gloria didn't make it a habit to visit Paul at the station. In fact, the last time she'd been there was during Andrea's murder investigation.

She stepped to the counter, the trash bag clutched in her right hand. "I'm looking for Paul Kennedy - if he's here."

The woman nodded. "Can I give him your name?"

Gloria nodded. "Tell him Gloria Rutherford would like to see him."

The woman disappeared through the side door.

Gloria stepped over to the corkboard on the sidewall. It was full of mugshots of wanted criminals. She remembered her recent arrest in

Tennessee. *At least one of them wasn't her mugshot.*

She shuddered at the memory of her one night in the slammer.

"And what do I owe the pleasure of this visit?"

Gloria's cheeks warmed as she whirled around and faced Paul. Her heart skipped a beat as her eyes settled on his crisp, dark uniform. "I'm glad I caught you," she said.

"Me too," he grinned.

Flustered by his flirting, Gloria glanced down at the trash bag in her hand. "I-I have something I think might be of interest in Dot's investigation."

He waved her back. "I would tell you that I'm surprised but I'm not," he teased.

She followed him as he led her to his now-familiar office. She took a seat near the door as he settled in behind the desk. He leaned back in the chair, his arms folded across his chest. "So what did you find?"

She slid the plastic bag in his direction. "We found this in the recycle bin behind Dot's restaurant."

Paul leaned forward in the chair. He opened the bag and peered inside before he glanced back at Gloria. "You found an empty bottle of toilet bowl cleaner?"

Gloria nodded.

"Is this Dot's?

She shook her head. "No. It's not. It was at the very top which means it was one of the last items tossed into the recycle bin the day of the poisoning."

"Did you touch it?" he asked.

She was proud of the fact that she had been smart enough not to touch what might be key evidence in the case. "No. I had gloves on when I picked it up," she explained.

He folded the top and set it off to the side. "I'll send it off to the lab for prints."

He went on. "Did you find anything else?"

"No," she answered. "I'm still working on suspects. What about you?"

"Not yet. We interviewed several witnesses but with no murder weapon, we were at a standstill in the case." He pointed at the garbage bag. "Until now, that is."

"I added Joe Toscani to my list. He's the owner of Pasta Amore."

Paul's eyebrows raised. "You went back there?"

She nodded sheepishly. "The girls and I ate dinner there tonight," she admitted. "I found out what his name was and then did a little research when I got home."

She didn't mention the food critic, how the critic had written a glowing review of the restaurant or the fact that the food critic and the owner were related. She wasn't sure how that angle tied in. Plus, she needed to do a bit more investigating.

"I better let you get back to work." Gloria got to her feet.

She started for the door. "Oh. We're still on for that cookout this Saturday."

"And your matchmaking?" Paul added.

Gloria's eyes twinkled. "I'm working on it."

He walked her to her car and gave her a quick peck on the cheek before opening the driver's side door.

Paul patted Mally's head before closing the door and leaning his head inside the open window. "Try to behave."

Gloria grinned. "I'll see what I can do."
With a small wave, she pulled away from the curb
and headed home.

The drive home took forever. Her eyelids
drooped as she tried to nod off behind the wheel.

She rolled the window down in an effort to
stay awake. It had been a hectic day and she was
plum wore out.

By the time she got home, she had just
enough energy to brush her teeth, pull on her
pajamas and climb into bed. Mally and Puddles
crawled in, with each taking up one side. She
was out within minutes.

Chapter Twelve

Gloria woke the next morning feeling energized and ready to tackle the day. She finished her morning routine before heading into town.

She could see lights on inside Dot's restaurant and there were cars parked out front.

Gloria eased Annabelle into an empty spot and climbed out of the car. She caught a glimpse of Dot darting back and forth beyond the front window as she scurried around the server station.

Gloria reached for the door handle. It was locked.

She shuffled to the window and pressed her face on the glass before tapping lightly.

Dot whirled around. A smile lit her face when she saw Gloria. There was a bounce in her step as she hurried to the front.

Dot unlocked the door and motioned her friend inside. "They've given us the all-clear to open the restaurant back up," she said.

Gloria hugged her friend. "I'm so glad."

Jennifer stepped out from the back holding a rag and glass cleaner. "We're back in business starting this afternoon."

"I'll be back for dinner," Gloria announced.

Dot would need all the support she could get. It was hard to guess what kind of response she would get from the locals. If anyone would show up...

Gloria turned to go. She needed to make her rounds to see if any of the other girls could join her for dinner.

She had a sudden thought. "Oh. Hey Jennifer. I'm having a cookout at my place Saturday at six. You and Tony and the kids are invited."

Jennifer wrinkled her nose. "Are you sure? My boys can eat a lot," she warned.

"Maybe we should turn it into a potluck," Dot chimed in. "Seems like you have a lot of people coming now."

Gloria nodded. Dot was right. The list was growing every day. "Yeah, maybe I should. I'll have hotdogs and hamburgers and maybe some of the other girls can bring a dish to pass."

She felt a little guilty about inviting people and then asking them to bring something, but she knew her friends wouldn't mind.

"I'll bring macaroni salad," Dot offered.

Gloria nodded. "That would be great." She made her way out the door, a mental list ticking off in her head.

She walked across the street and into the post office.

Ruth was the only one inside. She poked her head around the corner of the mailbox slots.

"Are you coming to my cookout Saturday night?" Gloria asked.

Ruth nodded. "I was planning on it."

"Somehow the list is growing and Dot thought it would be a good idea if we turned it into a potluck. Do you mind bringing some baked beans?"

"Of course not," Ruth replied. She stepped over to the counter. "Anything new on Dot's dilemma?"

"Nothing concrete. We're still working on it." Gloria glanced across the street in the direction of the restaurant. "They are opening for dinner. I thought it would be nice to show some support and eat there tonight. You wanna go with me?"

"Great minds think alike," Ruth said. "I already talked to Lucy and she's going to meet me there at six."

"I'll stop by Margaret's place on my way home and see if she can come, too." Gloria headed to the door. Today was shaping up to be as busy as yesterday.

Margaret's SUV was in the driveway. Gloria made her way to the breezeway door and pressed the doorbell. Westminster chimes echoed softly from within.

Moments later, Margaret pushed the door open. "You're up bright and early this morning."

Gloria laughed. "So are you."

"C'mon in. I was just getting ready to take my cup of coffee out on the back deck."

Margaret's home was beautiful, a sprawling ranch that faced Lake Terrace. Her friend had filled the home with trinkets she and her husband, Don, had picked up during their years of travel to exotic locales.

Gloria's favorite piece was a cross crucifix, hand carved from olive wood that she purchased on a trip to Jerusalem years ago.

Gloria had admired it so many times, Margaret told her she was going to wrap it up and gift it to her on her 80th birthday.

She followed Margaret into the kitchen where her friend poured two cups of coffee and handed one to Gloria. On the way out the slider door, she grabbed a piece of bread from a bread bag sitting on the kitchen table.

The deck was one of those expensive, new-fangled ones made from recycled materials that never faded or warped. It was a reddish earth tone color and large. It spanned the entire length of the rear of the house.

An expansive, sloping yard flowed from the deck down to the edge of the water. A few years back, Don constructed a wooden dock with a covered gazebo that jutted out into the water.

At the same time the dock went in, Don and Margaret hauled in dump trucks full of soft, white sand and they now had a powdery white beach.

Every summer they would throw a big backyard bash and invite half the town.

A plump mallard circled the dock before perching on the edge of the white sandy beach.

"That's Quack," Margaret told her. "He comes up here every morning to say hello." The duck waddled toward the house.

Margaret walked to the edge of the railing. She broke off small pieces of bread and tossed them in Quack's direction. He gobbled all the pieces before he waddled back down to the water's edge and floated off across the lake.

"You have a slice of paradise here," Gloria complimented.

Margaret settled back into her chair. "It is beautiful. The Lord sure has blessed us."

She changed the subject. "Anything new on Dot's case?"

Gloria told her how she had done some research on Joe Toscani and found out he was being investigated for his partner's murder in Chicago and there was mention of mob ties.

She also told her how Dot and she had met at the restaurant the night before and found the empty toilet cleaner inside the trash can.

Margaret gasped. "The police didn't find it?"

"Yeah," Gloria said. "That's what I thought. I turned it into Paul at the station. Maybe they'll find a fingerprint."

Gloria finished her cup of coffee and stood up. "I'm on my way to Gus's place. He had a run-in with Judith Arnett not too long ago."

Margaret was skeptical. "As much as I don't care for her, you don't really think she would try to kill Dot, do you?"

Gloria shrugged. She was leaning toward her not being the killer, but she wasn't ready to rule her out. Yet.

Margaret walked Gloria to her car. "Are you and Don coming over to my place Saturday night for the cookout?"

Margaret nodded. "Wouldn't miss it for the world," she said. "You need me to bring something?"

"If you don't mind. I hate to ask but it seems my list of invitees keeps growing. If it's not too much trouble, can you whip up a bowl of your famous creamy bacon and cheese potato salad?"

Margaret had a secret recipe for one of the best potato salads on the planet. Whenever Gloria tried to wheedle the recipe out of her,

Margaret refused. She explained that the recipe had passed down through the generations and she was sworn to secrecy.

Gloria tried a few times to imitate it. She came close but something was always missing.... Some key ingredient.

Margaret straightened her shoulders and lifted her head. "Of course I will. How many people did you invite?"

Gloria ticked off the mental list. Ruth, Liz, Lucy, Bill, Dot, Ray, Paul, Slick Steve, Margaret and Don, Al Dickerson. She was probably forgetting someone...Jennifer and Tony. "It looks like fourteen, unless I'm forgetting someone." She paused. "Andrea. I can't remember if I invited Andrea."

Gloria made a mental note to call her young friend when she got home before she hopped in the car and headed for Gus's shop.

When she reached the shop, Gloria parked off to the side and slid out of the driver's seat. She pushed open the front door and stepped into the outer office. The tinkling of the doorbell brought Gus from the back. He grinned when he spotted Gloria. "Hi Gloria."

Gus wasn't a tall guy. He was on the stocky side and his protruding belly was part of his charm. His hair was gray and thinning. He leaned an elbow on the small counter.

Gus and his wife, Mary Beth, lived in a small two-story house behind their automotive business. They had been a town fixture for over a decade now and as nice a couple as anyone could ever meet.

The last time Gloria had a problem with Annabelle's starter; Gus squeezed her in his schedule and fixed it in a jiffy.

He even loaned her his own vehicle so she would have a way to get around. On top of that, he gave her a discount.

He pulled off his ball cap and scratched the top of his head. "Annabelle giving you a hard time?"

Gloria shook her head and stepped closer to the counter. "No. She's running like a top, thanks to you."

"I'm here for another reason." She glanced around the small office. "You heard about Dot's restaurant?"

Gus rubbed the stubble on his chin thoughtfully. "Yeah. What a shame."

Gloria went on. "Dot had a run-in with Judith Arnett just days before the poisoning."

Gus's mouth twisted in a grim frown. "You don't say..."

"I heard you had a problem with her not long ago."

Gus nodded. "Sure did." He walked around the edge of the counter and came to stand out front. "She was in here snooping around. Not that she was having vehicle trouble or anything. Just being her usual nosy self."

The bell on the front of the shop chimed. As luck would have it, it was Carl Arnett, Judith's husband.

"Hi Carl. I'll be right with you," Gus said. He motioned Gloria to the back of the repair shop. They moved off to the side, out of earshot.

He lowered his voice. "She started talking trash. How she heard rumors of marital problems between Mary Beth and me. I told her to stop spreading vicious rumors that weren't true. Then I asked her to leave and told her to never step foot on my property or I would have her arrested for trespassing.

Gus smirked. "She stormed out of the shop and peeled out of the parking lot. Had her madder than a wet hornet."

Gloria smiled at the mental image of Gus putting Judith in her place.

"Next thing I know, customers are coming in here, telling me Judith was spreading vicious rumors that she caught me sipping out of a paper bag here in the back." Gus shifted his feet. "You know that's not true."

Gloria reached out and touched his arm. "I know Gus. No one in Belhaven believes half. No – most - of what Judith says," she reassured him.

Gus nodded his head in the direction of Judith's husband, still waiting out in the front lobby. "I don't have a beef with Carl - but his wife? She's not welcome here anymore."

Gloria thanked Gus for his time. She turned to go when she noticed the car perched on the hoist. It looked familiar. She pointed up. "That looks like Jennifer's car."

Gus nodded. "Yeah. She has been having trouble with it lately. I feel sorry for her and Tony. What with his hours cut back at the shop and her being off for a few days since Dot's place has been shut down."

She avoided facing Carl as she made her way out through the large overhead garage door. Gus didn't tell her anything about Judith she didn't already know. She was a gossip and thief. Still, those two characteristics didn't make her a killer.

When she got home, she dialed Paul's number, hoping he had news on the toilet bowl cleaner. She left a message on his cell phone. He was probably home sleeping.

Gloria whipped up a tossed salad, keeping in mind that she was eating dinner at Dot's later. She slid into a kitchen chair and tapped on the side of her salad plate as she glanced at the coins in her kitchen. It sure would be nice to find out if the girls would be allowed to keep them.

She finished her salad and then headed to her computer in the corner of the dining room. It was time to work on finding a good attorney.

She soon discovered there were tons of attorneys in the area. Half an hour later, she had narrowed it down to three and set up appointments for later in the week.

Relieved she was working on her end of the research, she swept the kitchen floor and then the back porch before settling into the porch rocker.

Mally followed her outside and darted back and forth across the yard, sniffing the flowering bushes that lined the side of the house and then chasing after the squirrels.

Gloria rocked back and forth in the chair. Her mind drifted to the investigation and her discoveries so far.

Joe Toscani was a prime suspect with Judith being a close second. Toscani had more motive than Judith did, although Judith also had a motive...revenge.

Gloria decided to head down to the restaurant a little before official opening time. She wanted to lend Dot a hand in the back, if needed.

She also figured Dot might need a little moral support or an encouraging word.

Gloria turned onto the alley and parked next to Dot's van.

She hurried to the rear entrance and slipped in the back door. Jennifer was there, chopping veggies for house salads. "I'm surprised to see you here, Jennifer," Gloria said. "Where's your car?"

Jennifer scooped up the sliced tomatoes and dumped them into a large bowl. "I don't know what's going on with it lately. First, I had a tire blowout a couple weeks ago. Yesterday, the brakes went out."

Dot wandered into the back. "She almost got into a serious accident. Drove right through the stop sign here on Main Street."

Dot stuck the mustard and ketchup containers on a large serving tray and headed back out front. "Good thing no one was coming from the other direction. Otherwise, she could've gotten killed."

Gloria remembered Gus's shop. "That's right. I saw your car out at Gus's place."

Gloria stopped to hug Jennifer. "I'm glad you're okay."

She rounded the corner of the prep area and found Dot bouncing from table-to-table, arranging the condiments as if it were some sort of culinary contest.

"You think anyone is going to show up for dinner?" she fretted.

"All the girls are coming. That makes at least half a dozen of us."

215

Dot grabbed the edge of her plain brown apron and began twisting it in her hands. Gloria's heart went out to her. Poor thing was nervous as a tick.

She needed to stay busy and stop worrying. Gloria grabbed her arm and tugged. "Let's go to the back and help Jennifer."

Gloria cleaned the pass thru window on her way to the kitchen. She glanced at a paper on top of the pile. It looked like some sort of contract. "I hate to be nosy, Dot." Gloria pulled it close to her face. "What's this?"

"You mean that legal-looking thingy?"

Gloria grabbed her glasses from her purse and slipped them on. She scanned the sheet. "This is an offer to buy the restaurant?"

Gloria looked at Dot. "Are you thinking about selling?" She knew Dot was distressed over the death but didn't think she was serious about selling.

Ray rounded the corner right. "Brian Sellers keeps sending us offers to buy the place," he explained.

Brian Sellers owned the small grocery store on the corner. He also owned the drug store and hardware store. If he bought Dot's place, he would own half of Main Street.

Dot grabbed the stack from Gloria's hand. "He sends us an offer about once a month now. Each time, he ups the price a little more. I think he's getting desperate," she decided.

"Do you think he's desperate enough to poison someone and drive you out of business?"

Dot and Ray looked at each other uneasily. The thought hadn't occurred to them.

Brian Sellers was a bit of a mystery around town. He had moved to Belhaven less than a year ago, into one of the larger homes on Lake Terrace.

Before he moved in, he gutted the place, all the way down to the studs. Gloria had never been inside, but rumor had it he'd spent a small fortune turning it into a state-of-the-art bachelor pad, complete with bowling alley and indoor pool.

Gloria heard that at one time, he had some business dealings with Andrea's dead husband, Daniel, and his illegal gambling business.

The gambling business had gone belly up when Daniel died and his partner, Barry Hicks, was convicted of murder and sent to prison.

Andrea had continued to run the insurance agency and was doing quite well with it.

"You don't think he's going to try to start a gambling business here in town?" Gloria voiced her concerns.

She thought of something else. "Was Sellers in the restaurant the morning of the poisoning?"

Jennifer shook her head. "Nope. I didn't see him. He always parks his SUV at the far end of the alley, close to hardware store. I think he hangs out there a lot," she added.

Dot swallowed hard and glanced at the clock. "Time to unlock the doors."

Ray squeezed her arm before heading to the front to turn the sign over. "We can do this," he told his wife.

Dot cleared her throat as she eyed the front entrance.

Ray turned the sign and unlocked the front door. Half a dozen town folk followed him through the door.

Dot breathed a sigh of relief. People were coming back.

Soon, the entire restaurant was packed and a line of diners waited for an empty table.

Gloria's chest swelled with pride. This was what it meant to live in a small town, where everyone looked out for one another, supported them and loved them.

The rest of the evening was a blur. Gloria worked behind the scenes helping Dot and Ray. She bussed tables, ran the cash register and even delivered glasses of water to the tables.

Halfway through dinner service, Gloria noticed Brian Sellers and another man as they walked in the front door. They made their way over to a small booth in the corner.

Gloria grabbed two waters, a couple menus and headed in their direction. She didn't recognize the man with Brian Sellers, who was older and closer to Gloria's age.

When she reached the table, she got a good look at him. He looked familiar but she couldn't place the face.

She set a glass of water in front of each of them and placed the menus next to the water. "Your server will be right with you." The men nodded.

Gloria strode toward the back. It was then she had an idea. For the next hour, she kept a sharp eye on the table and the two men.

As soon as they paid and exited the restaurant, she made a beeline for the cluttered table. She pulled a clean napkin from her pocket and carefully picked up Brian Sellers' fork by the tines.

She dropped the fork into a plastic to-go container. Next, she picked up his water glass, holding onto it by the very bottom and then carried that and the to-go container to the back.

Dot was at the sink rinsing dishes. She reached for the dirty glass. "Here, I'll take that," she offered.

"No! I mean. No. This is Brian Sellers' water glass. I'm taking it to Paul to have him check for fingerprints."

Dot wiped her hands on a towel as Ray wandered in.

Gloria showed them the to-go container with the fork inside. "I'm going to see if Paul can check for a match with the toilet bowl cleaner," she explained.

Ray snapped his fingers. "Brilliant idea. Too bad we can't track down the prints for any of the other suspects."

"Joe Toscani, the owner of Pasta Amore, has a criminal record," she reminded them. "His prints are on file and Paul is already checking to see if it's a match."

Gloria slipped the glass and fork into a plastic bag and set them off to the side, right next to her purse. "Now we need to get Judith's prints. Somehow."

"I bet Ruth could get it," Dot said.

Gloria slapped her forehead in an "aha" moment. "That's a great idea." She headed straight for the dining.

Lucy and Ruth were sharing a piece of cheesecake.

Gloria pulled out a chair and plopped down next to them. "I need a favor, Ruth."

Ruth could tell by the look on Gloria's face it was something good. She leaned forward. "What?"

Gloria glanced around. "I need Judith Arnett's fingerprints," Gloria whispered.

Ruth leaned back in the chair. "That's all? I can have them for you tomorrow," she boasted. "Judith comes in every morning around nine."

"I'll be there before noon to pick them up," Gloria promised. "And remember. Keep 'em clean, as in don't contaminate it with your own prints."

Ruth looked deeply offended. "Of course. I know better than that."

Lucy leaned in. "You really think Judith is capable of murder?"

"I'm not ruling her out. Yet."

Gloria caught a glimpse of Dot pacing back and forth near the server station. "Look, I gotta get back there." She jumped to her feet and headed to the rear.

"What's wrong Dot?" Gloria asked.

"I lost my glasses." Dot stopped in her tracks. She stuck her hand on her hip. "I had them just a minute ago."

Gloria grinned. She reached up and tapped Dot's forehead. The glasses fell down and landed on Dot's nose.

The two women burst out laughing. "Oh my. I'm so glad this night is almost over," Dot groaned.

Gloria was, too. It had been a huge success and she was happy for Dot and Ray. Half an hour later, Ray turned the sign in the front window to *Closed* and locked the door after the last customer left.

The four of them – Dot, Ray, Gloria and Jennifer wandered into the kitchen. Everything was neat and tidy. They were ready to start a new day the next morning.

Dot grabbed some clean plates from an overhead shelf. She carved out four pieces of leftover lasagna from the last remaining pan. She plucked a piece of garlic bread from the warming tray, placed it on the plate beside the lasagna and handed it to Jennifer. Next, she handed a plate of food to Gloria.

She finished two more plates and the foursome made their way to an empty table near the front.

As they ate dinner, they discussed the resounding success of the re-opening of Dot's place.

Tears filled Dot's eyes. "I-I can't believe how many people turned out tonight."

Gloria cut off a piece of lasagna. She paused before putting the delicious cheesy pasta into her mouth. "I'm not the least bit surprised. This town loves you and we can't live without you."

The subject turned to the investigation. Gloria told the group that Ruth would get a set of

Judith's fingerprints in the morning and then she was going to take those and Brian Sellers's prints to the police station to be tested.

The group carried their empty plates to the kitchen, washed and dried them and then put them away.

Dot and Ray locked the back door before they all headed to their vehicles.

Gloria turned to Jennifer. "I can give you a ride home," she offered.

Jennifer nodded. "That would be great. Otherwise, I can just call Tony."

Gloria shook her head. "No problem." They waved goodnight to Ray and Dot and climbed into Annabelle.

"I can't wait to get my car back," Jennifer confessed. "This is such a pain having to hitch rides or wait for Tony to come get me."

Gloria didn't get out of the car at Jennifer's place. Instead, she waited 'til Jennifer was safely inside her house before she backed out of the driveway.

Mally was waiting just inside the door when Gloria opened it. She patted her head as Puddles wandered over and wound himself around Gloria's legs. She was exhausted. More than anything, she wanted to sit down and relax.

Gloria grabbed a bag of potato chips, poured a tall glass of cold lemonade and headed to the living room.

It was still early and she had plenty of time to watch a couple episodes of her favorite whodunit series, "Detective on the Side."

She slid into the recliner and popped the footrest out before turning the television on.

It was heavenly to kick back and relax for a change. The days had been so hectic, there were times she wasn't sure if she was coming or going.

Tomorrow would be another busy one in between dropping off the fingerprints for testing, visiting the attorneys to discuss possible wills and stopping at the grocery to pick up supplies for her upcoming cookout.

She munched on the salty potato chips as she watched her show, an episode she had never seen.

Joyce Jameson, the female detective, was tracking down a killer who stalked women at rest areas off busy highways. They used Joyce as a decoy. She barely made it out alive after her backup was stuck in an accident on the freeway and she had to fight off the killer by herself.

Gloria jotted down her grocery list during commercials and by the time the show was over, she'd eaten half a bag of chips - but at least she had finished her list.

She struggled to keep her eyes open for the 11:00 news but gave up just as it came on the air.

Gloria wandered into the bathroom, brushed her teeth, pulled on her pajamas and headed to bed.

Chapter Thirteen

Gloria started a pot of coffee and wandered out onto the porch to grab the newspaper that was in her driveway. She settled into the porch rocker as Mally galloped around the yard and stretched her legs.

There was nothing earth shattering in the headlines. The topic of the month, other than the death at Dot's place, was that their small town was getting a stop light to replace the current stop sign.

Gloria thought the whole thing a waste of money. The stop sign worked just fine. A stop light was major overkill. Plus, she thought it took away from the charm of their small town.

Still, no one could stand in the way of progress so she decided she might as well just accept the fact that change, however small, was headed to Belhaven.

She opened the paper and scanned the pages. She spied a picture of the now-familiar food critic. What was her name? Gloria squinted but the whole thing was a blur. She opened the porch door, reached inside and grabbed her glasses off the table. She popped them back on and opened the paper back up.

Gloria almost wished she hadn't. Her heart sank when she caught the critic's headline. "Disappointment at Dot's." The write up was short, just three or four paragraphs – but the damage couldn't have been any worse.

Amy Martola described how she ate at Dot's the night the restaurant reopened. She made a point of mentioning the food poisoning and that the case was still under investigation.

Gloria felt her blood begin to boil as the woman wrote about mediocre lasagna and stale garlic bread. She even mentioned her Diet Coke was flat and alluded to the fact that they must not clean the soda machines often.

Gloria slapped the paper on her lap. She had a good mind to call Amy Martola's boss and tell them she was related to the owner of Pasta Amore and was targeting Dot's restaurant, Pasta Amore's only real competition for miles around.

She stormed into the house and slammed the door. It was then she remembered Mally was still outside.

She opened the door, stuck her head outside and hollered. "C'mon girl. Time to come in."

Still seething, she grabbed the phone and started to dial the number on the "contact us" portion of the paper. She hung up just as the line started to ring. It wasn't her place to fight Dot's battle. What if Dot didn't want her help?

Ratting out the reviewer would make Gloria feel better, but might put an even bigger target on the restaurant's back.

No. The best thing she could do for Dot was find the killer - or killers - and bring them to justice.

Gloria was chomping at the bit to get the fingerprints in for testing. She held off until 10:30 before she hopped in the car and headed to the post office.

The parking lot was packed. She eased into a spot on the end and made her way inside.

Ruth was busy at the counter. She waved her to the side. Gloria waited for Ruth to wrap up her conversation before making her way to the counter. "Did you get it?" she whispered loudly.

Ruth rolled her eyes and pounded her fist on the counter. "No. She didn't touch a stinkin' thing."

"I tried, Gloria. I tried. I even asked her to check out our new book of stamps," she said "The ones with the picture of the Great Lakes."

"The harder I tried, the more determined she was not to. It was almost as if she knew what I was trying to do."

Gloria's heart sank. She needed a print. "Don't worry about it, Ruth. Like my mother used to say, *there's more than one way to skin a cat.*"

She headed back to her car. There was only one way to get a print...from Judith's own house.

Judith and Carl lived a block back from Main Street in a tidy, one-story ranch. The house had a decent-sized yard but neighbors were near enough to keep an eye on the coming and goings of one another.

Gloria rolled past the house and white picket fence that framed the front yard. She spied Judith's Ford Taurus parked in front of the garage. The door to the small metal shed out back was wide open.

A sudden movement caught her eye. Judith was on the side of the house pruning her prize rose bushes.

Judith had a green thumb. She entered her pink heirloom roses in Montbay County Fair every year and almost every single time, she won. The only reason Gloria knew this was that Judith made a point of bringing her ribbons into Dot's restaurant after she won.

She loved to rub it in the faces of others who entered the contest and never even placed.

Gloria backed Annabelle into the drive of the house that was catty-corner to Judith's house. The place was for sale and had been vacant since the previous fall.

She pulled far enough back so her car was not visible from Judith's line of vision. She eased out of the car and tiptoed around the side, careful to stay hidden from view.

The lawn was overgrown and weeds ruled the neglected property. Gloria prayed no critters were lurking nearby as she peeked around the edge.

Judith had moved. She was working on a bed of flowers in front of her picture window. Gloria was close enough to hear her humming to herself as she snipped and clipped.

A thought popped into Gloria's head. *Hadn't someone mentioned Judith was on crutches and had sprained her ankle?*

Judith's head snapped up and she stared right at Gloria.

Gloria yanked her head back. Her heart started to pound. She was certain that Judith had seen her. She stood motionless for a full minute; convinced Judith was on her way over.

She never materialized so Gloria eased her head forward for another glance. Judith was nowhere in sight. The shed doors were closed.

Gloria stood ramrod straight and leaned flat against the rear of the house. *If only she could get her hands on those pruning shears,* she thought.

A car door slammed. The sound of a car engine drifted across the street.

Could she get this lucky? She whipped her head around, just in time to see Judith back her sedan out of the driveway and pull out onto the street.

Her golden opportunity to snatch the shears was at hand. She pulled a clean tissue from her purse and bolted down the driveway.

Gloria jogged across the street and followed the fence line along the back of Judith's property.

She prayed none of Judith's neighbors were watching her through their curtains.

Her heart thumped in her chest and her brow began to sweat. Her hand trembled as she twisted the knob on the metal shed and pulled the creaky door open.

There, hanging on a hook near the door, were the pruning shears. Gloria grabbed the edge of the metal tip and slid them off. She eased the metal door shut and headed for the fence.

Gloria had almost cleared the property when she spied Carl Arnett's truck coming from the opposite direction.

She did an about-face and prayed Carl hadn't noticed her. She darted behind the neighbor's house and out of sight.

Gloria waited for Carl to get out of his truck and go inside the house before she sprinted through the yard and across the street to her car.

She yanked the back door open and laid the clippers on the seat, careful not to touch anything but the tip of the shear.

Gloria slid in the front seat, started the car and stepped on the gas as she tore out of the driveway. On the way to the corner, she passed Judith.

Mission accomplished, she headed out of town toward Montbay Police Department.

Chapter Fourteen

Paul stared at the pruning shears, fork and water glass. "Who did you say these belong to?"

"The pruning shears are Judith Arnett's, the woman who tried to steal from Dot's restaurant just days before the murder," she patiently explained, and then pointed at the fork and glass. "Those two belong to Brian Sellers."

"He is my latest suspect. I found out he's buying up all the real estate on Belhaven's Main Street and now he wants to buy Dot's place. He keeps sending her offers."

Paul leaned on his desktop and propped his chin in his fist. "That doesn't mean he's a killer."

"Dot isn't going to sell. He's been hounding her for months now. Maybe he hoped she would change her mind if business dropped off after someone died eating the food," she theorized.

A light tap on the door interrupted the conversation. A woman poked her head inside. "Detective Osborne is here to see you."

Gloria slid out of the chair. "I'll decide on him one way or the other after tonight," she said.

Great, Paul thought. It was exactly what he hoped wouldn't happen. "Let me guess. You're going to stake out his place."

She shook her head. "No. I'm going to take a more direct approach this time. I'm going to walk right up to his front door and ask him point-blank."

"Ask him what?"

"If he poisoned Mike Foley in the restaurant," she explained. "You know. The element of surprise. Maybe I can catch him off guard."

Paul rubbed the back of his neck. "That's a different strategy," he acknowledged.

He walked her to the front lobby. "Give me a call after you get home so I know you're safe."

Paul tipped her head forward and kissed the top. He held the door open and she stepped outside.

It was at that precise moment, he dropped a bomb. "We have a suspect."

Gloria spun around. "You do? Who is it?"

He shook his head. "I can't say yet."

"Can you tell me if it's someone I already mentioned?"

"It's not."

Gloria clenched her fists and shook them in the air. "Ohhh. This is going to drive me crazy," she said. "Do I know the suspect?"

Paul nodded. "Yes and for everyone's sake, I hope we're wrong."

Gloria grabbed the handrail and took a step down. Her head was spinning. *Someone she hadn't considered yet. Someone she knew?*

She reached the bottom step before coming to an abrupt halt. What if police suspected Dot's husband, Ray?

She shook her head and dismissed the thought. No way was it Ray. He had opportunity - but what about motive?

Why would the police suspect him? Were his prints on the empty toilet bowl cleaner? Gloria's hand flew to her mouth. That was it. They had his prints on the empty container.

She wandered into the road and the path of an oncoming car. The driver laid on the horn.

Gloria clutched her chest as she jumped out of the way. She mouthed the words "sorry" and scooted the rest of the way across the street.

A stop at the first of three attorneys was next on her list.

After the first meeting, Gloria had a greater appreciation for putting one's wishes in a will so that someday down the road – after she was gone – what she intended to leave for her children and grandchildren wouldn't end up tied up in the courts for years.

She made it to the other two attorney appointments, careful to ask questions and take notes.

After the final meeting, Gloria decided, at least for herself, to go with the first attorney. It was a woman, Patricia Caldwell. Not that they all hadn't appeared competent and knowledgeable. She felt she related best to her.

Maybe because she seemed more personable. The fact that she had several pictures of her grandchildren displayed on her desk and her credenza gave Gloria a good feeling.

She had one more stop to make - Brian Sellers's house. She drove to the edge of town, and Nails and Knobs, the hardware store on the corner, caught her attention.

Gloria pulled into an empty spot in front and slid out. She needed propane for her gas grill and the cookout was only a couple days away. She could kill two birds with one stone if the owner, Brian Sellers, was inside.

She climbed the single step and pushed open the antique glass door. The inside of the place hadn't changed in over 30 years. If anything, it was more charming than ever.

The original hardwood floors creaked lightly as Gloria made her way down the center aisle.

To Gloria, the best thing about the store were the odds and ends, bits and pieces. There was a little of everything, stuff the newer, big box stores never carried. At least the new owner, Mr. Sellers, kept the store close to its original charm, and why wouldn't he? The store did a brisk business, even in a town as small as Belhaven.

She spied her target straight ahead. He was behind a long wooden counter, ringing up a roll of porch screen.

Gloria glanced from side to side as she made her way to the back. There were buckets of bolts, bins of door hinges. A sign above the cash register said, "We cut glass."

The customer grabbed his screen and sidestepped Gloria as he passed her on the way out.

She studied the young man as she moved closer. He didn't look like a cold-blooded killer. His cropped, jet-black hair stuck straight up – as if he jelled it that way.

It reminded her of the goop her mom used to use when she rolled her hair. What was it called? Dippity Do.

He watched Gloria approach the counter. His intense blue eyes were striking. If she had to guess, she would say he was in his early 30's. "Can I help you?"

"Yes. I need a propane tank for my gas grill," Gloria explained.

"Yes, ma'am. I can take care of that for you. Do you need anything else?" he asked.

Before she could change her mind, Gloria blurted out. "You're the one trying to buy Dot's restaurant."

Brian Sellers placed his elbows on the counter and gazed at Gloria. "Yes ma'am. I am," he admitted.

"You heard about the poisoning." It was a statement, not a question.

"An unfortunate accident," he said.

"Say. You look familiar." He snapped his fingers. "You're the woman that's a bit of a legend around here. The lady detective that catches the criminal every time." His eyes narrowed. "Gloria something."

"Rutherford," she said. "Gloria Rutherford."

"Oh...now I see." He straightened back up. "You're here because you think *I'm* a suspect."

Brian Sellers shoved his hands in his front pockets and rocked back on his heels. "Do I look like a killer?" he asked.

"No," she admitted.

"Are you sure?" His eyes twinkled as he choked back a laugh. "Don't you want to interrogate me?"

He leaned his elbows on the counter again and crossed his arms. "Ask me anything. Anything at all."

Gloria could have been offended. Maybe she should have been offended, but she wasn't. Instead, he was entertaining her.

She plopped her purse on the counter and hopped up on an empty barstool. "Since you offered..."

He held up a finger. "Can I get you a cup of coffee before we get started?" He didn't wait for an answer as he grabbed two cups off the shelf behind him.

He poured the coffee and slid one across the counter toward Gloria. "Cream or sugar?"

Gloria grabbed that handle. "No thanks. I like mine black."

"Me too," he agreed. "So back to my interrogation. Do you want to know where I was the morning of the murder?"

He took a sip of coffee, set it down and tapped his lip, as if in deep thought. "I walked my dog early. Around six a.m., I think. Then I came here to work. I opened around eight, I guess."

"What kind of dog?" Gloria interrupted.

"Is he a suspect too?" Brian shot back.

Gloria grinned. "No." The man had a way of putting her at ease. He was teasing her, but in a good way.

"Finn is a great Dane and a big baby. Sometimes I let him come to work with me," he confided.

He went on. "I took a lunch break somewhere between 11:30 and noon. I went home to let Finn out. I warmed up some leftovers and then came back here."

"I heard you have a beautiful home," she said.

"Stop by sometime. I'll give you a tour," he offered.

Gloria took a sip of coffee and changed the subject. "What did you do before you moved to Belhaven and started buying up our small town?"

Mr. Sellers wrapped his hands around the cup. He took a drink as he studied Gloria over the rim. "I was a circuit court judge."

"A judge?" Her eyes narrowed suspiciously. He looked too young to have been a judge. It was as if he read her mind.

"One of the youngest judges in the State of Michigan," he said. "And I'm not as young as I look."

"Well I'll be darned." She sighed. "I guess I'll have to rule you out as suspect."

"Judges can be killers, too," he pointed out.

He almost seemed disappointed. "Does that mean you don't have any more questions for me?"

Gloria swallowed the last drop of coffee and set the cup on his side of the counter. "No. It appears you're off the hook. I still need that tank of propane, though."

He grabbed her empty cup and set it in the sink along with his before he turned back around to ring up her purchase. "I'll meet you out front."

She wandered back through the store and waited on the sidewalk. She opened the rear car door as Brian slid the heavy metal tank onto the floor.

He stood. "I was serious about the tour."

Gloria nodded. "I would like that."

She tilted her head and gazed into the brightest blue eyes she had ever seen. Her heart fluttered. If she were decades younger – several decades -, he would be on her radar.

She narrowed her eyes. Attractive. Single. She glanced down to confirm the lack of a wedding ring. Hardworking. He would be a real catch for the right girl... "Say, what are you doing Saturday night?"

"This Saturday?"

Gloria nodded.

"Finn and I haven't made any plans yet." That confirmed his single status.

Gloria opened the driver's side door. "I'm having a cookout at my place Saturday around six. Would you like to come?"

"As long as you don't pressure Dot and her husband Ray to sell their place," she warned.

"Sure." Brian grinned. He made an "X" across his chest and then held up three fingers. "I promise to behave. Scout's honor."

She recited her address. "Do you want to write the address down?"

"No. I think I've got it." A small frown shadowed his face. "Are you sure you want me there? Dot and Ray won't mind?"

"Yes. I'm sure. I think you'll fit in quite well with our group." She slid into the driver's seat and gave a small wave as she backed out of the parking spot.

He seemed like such a nice, young man. Ambitious, funny, handsome. Her eyebrows furrowed briefly.

Paul would think she was double-matchmaking. First Liz and now Andrea. Oh well. Nothing ventured, nothing gained.

She made a mental note to stop inviting people to the cookout. The list was getting out of hand.

Chapter Fifteen

The rest of the week flew by. She spent Thursday morning with Jill and the boys. They wandered up and down the aisles at the flea market.

Most of the stuff was just junk but there were also a few treasures, including an old metal milk carton. Gloria decided it would be perfect for turning into a flowerpot for her porch.

There was one brief mishap when Ryan, her youngest grandson, came up missing. They spent a good hour searching the crowded aisles for the stinker.

On her second trip around the place, Gloria paused. *If I were a young boy, where would I go?* she wondered.

She headed to the animal auction building. There was no sign of him.

Her eyes scanned the rows of sellers peddling their wares. Off in the far corner was a small cluster of Amish buggies.

The Amish were there every week, selling baked goods and homemade quilts. They did a brisk business. Who could resist homemade baked goods? Her eyes narrowed. *Not a young boy.*

Gloria made a beeline for the buggies. She spied a pair of sneakers – familiar sneakers – poking out next to a large, spoked wheel. She crossed her arms. "Ryan Adams. Come out here this instant."

The feet disappeared and a blonde head peeked out from the black frame. "Hi Grams." She knelt down. On closer inspection, she noticed his face was covered with chunks of chocolate and dried vanilla icing. An empty wrapper was on the ground next to him. "Where did you get that?"

His blonde head twisted wildly. "They gave it to me."

"Who gave it to you?"

"One of the ladies with a white hat." Gloria glanced up. All of the Amish women wore white hair coverings.

She made her way around the side of the buggy where a small cluster of women stood.

Ryan followed behind. A sticky hand reached for hers and her heart melted. She looked down. Large, innocent eyes met hers. *How could she stay mad at a face like that?* She squeezed his hand.

"My grandson, here, seems to have enjoyed one of your baked goods. He said someone gave it to him."

A young Amish girl, who couldn't have been more than twelve years old, stepped forward. "I-I hope you don't mind." She glanced down at Ryan who held Gloria's hand in a tight grip. "He said he was hungry...and lost."

Gloria shook her head. "That's fine, dear. I just wanted to thank you and make sure we don't owe you for the treats." She opened her purse and pulled out her wallet.

The girl reached out her hand to stop her. "No, ma'am. No charge." Gloria closed her purse. "Thank you."

She ruffled Ryan's hair as they walked off in search of Jill and Tyler, who were headed their way.

The rest of the afternoon flew by and before she knew it, Jill and the boys were gone.

***

By the time Saturday – the day of the cookout - rolled around, Gloria was in a semi-state of panic. She was feverishly working on her Oreo cookie cream dessert when she heard a light tap on the porch door. Gloria flung the door open. It was Andrea. "I'm here to help."

Her eyes shot heavenward. "Thank God."

Gloria wasted no time. She grabbed her young friend's arm and pulled her inside. "How did you know?"

She dropped an apron over her head and promptly put her to work slicing tomatoes, chopping onions and assembling hamburger patties.

Andrea frowned at the tower of hamburger patties. "How many people did you invite?"

Gloria wiped her hands on the front of her apron. She grabbed a head of cabbage and a sharp knife from the wooden butcher block.

With expert precision, she chopped the cabbage down the center. "I lost count."

Paul arrived next. She sent him back outside to set up tables and folding chairs under the big oak tree in the back of the yard.

Margaret and Don arrived, followed by Dot and Ray. Lucy and Bill were close behind. By the time Gloria hung up her apron, she had a full house and Paul was doing an excellent job entertaining the guests.

She peeked through the edge of the curtains and smiled with pride. Even though he'd never met half of the guests that were there, he acted as if he'd known them for years. Yes, he fit in the small town of Belhaven quite nicely.

Slick Steve was next. He stood off to the side uncertainly. Gloria started to head outside to greet him when Liz wandered over. She watched as Liz pulled him into the crowd.

The last to arrive to the party was Brian Sellers. He parked his dark blue SUV at the end of the row of cars, near the road. He was getting a good bit of attention, especially from Dot and Ray. With everything going on, she hadn't had a chance to tell them he was coming.

She wove her way around her guests and came up next to him. "I'm glad you could make it, Brian."

His blue eyes crinkled at the corner. "You sure know how to throw a shin-dig."

"Just a few friends from town." She reached for his arm. "Come on. What would you like to drink — iced tea or lemonade?"

"Lemonade please."

They made their way to the top of the porch where Paul was standing. Brian's hand shot out. "Hi. I'm Brian. Brian Sellers."

Paul shook his hand. "Paul Kennedy."

Gloria poured a lemonade and handed him the glass.

Paul rubbed his chin. "You look familiar."

"I own the hardware store in town?" he offered.

"Maybe you saw him around the courthouse. This is former judge Brian Sellers," Gloria said.

"That's where I've seen you."

Gloria excused herself and started her rounds, chatting with guests. She was pleased to see that Liz and Al Dickerson were deep in conversation.

Liz grabbed Gloria's arm as she walked by. "Gloria, I didn't know you knew Al. We used to work together years ago at the paper mill."

"Well, isn't that a coincidence..."

Paul wandered by with an armful of trash. Gloria followed him into the kitchen. "Let me take care of those." She felt guilty for putting him to work.

He handed her a stack of glasses, all except for one. She reached for it.

He pulled it back and shook his head. "I need to hang onto this one."

Gloria frowned and shifted her gaze. He wanted the glass for the fingerprints. "You can put it back in the bedroom," she quietly replied.

She watched him disappear into the other room and then turned to gaze outside. A warm spring breeze drifted through the window as Gloria stared out at her guests and waited for Paul to return.

One of her guests was a suspect. Her eyes wandered to Ray, who was standing next to Dot. He tipped his head back and chuckled at something Bill or Lucy had just said. *Poor Dot. I wonder if she knows...*

Paul returned to the kitchen. He pulled the fridge door open, reached inside and lifted the tall tray of burgers from the shelf.

Gloria came in behind him and grabbed the packs of hot dogs. She followed him out to the grill. "Thanks, love." He planted a kiss on her forehead and fired up the grill.

Margaret met her on the porch. "Can I help?" Gloria forced a smile. *Surely, Margaret wasn't a suspect...* "That would be wonderful."

The girls arranged large bowls of potato and macaroni salad, a crockpot full of baked beans and Gloria's homemade coleslaw on the serving table. Stacks of hamburger and hotdog buns along with mustard, ketchup, onions and pickles followed.

By the time the girls had arranged all the food, Paul and Ray were on their way over with the cooked burgers and dogs.

The guests assembled around the table.

"Let's say grace." Paul offered a solemn prayer of thanks for the food and fellowship.

Gloria lifted her head. Ray was standing across from her. *I wonder if this is his last meal as a free man,* she wondered. She added a silent prayer investigators would find him innocent. If she had to pick a guilty party, she would choose Judith Arnett over Ray any day.

Paul and Gloria stood off to the side as they watched guests load their plates with goodies. "Did you find a print match for Judith or Joe Toscani?" She already knew the answer. If there had been a match, he wouldn't be after Ray's cup.

Paul shook his head. "The results won't be back until Monday."

That was something. Gloria held out a glimmer of hope that it would be one of them...

They joined the end of the line. Neither of them had eaten all day.

Gloria grabbed a hotdog and hamburger, shifted them to the side and then scooped a large spoonful of each of the sides onto the empty space on her plate.

She followed Paul to the last two seats, which were right next to Andrea and Brian Sellers. Andrea was laughing at something Brian had just said.

"The food is delicious Mrs. Rutherford," Brian complimented.

"Thank you, Brian. I'm so glad you could make it."

She bit into her hotdog thoughtfully. *What if the cup Paul kept belonged to Brian instead? That couldn't be it. She had already given him Brian's prints.*

She gave Paul a sideways glance. He was stone-faced. His expression gave nothing away.

Andrea picked up a chip and paused. "Brian grew up in New York, just like me."

267

Paul settled his hand on his leg and studied Brian. "So what brought you to the small town of Belhaven?"

Brian grabbed the paper napkin tucked under his plate and wiped the corners of his mouth. "My grandparents. Actually, their house brought me here. The house on Lake Terrace was theirs. I inherited it."

Gloria tilted her head and gazed at Brian. She knew little about the elderly couple that had resided in the lakeside house. They had always been a bit of a mystery.

He went on. "I came for a visit to settle the estate and fell in love with the area. Small town life seemed to fit me," he said.

"Me too," Andrea said.

The chemistry between the two was obvious. He seemed like such a nice, young man. What if they started dating and later found out he was the killer? Andrea's life would be turned upside down once again. It would be Gloria's fault for playing matchmaker...

Gloria grabbed her empty plate and headed to the trashcan.

Paul was right behind her. "You invited Brian Sellers to this get-together for Andrea."

She whirled around. "Yeah and if he ends up being the killer, I'm going to feel terrible," she admitted.

She glanced back at the two, still sitting side-by-side. Andrea tilted her head forward as she eagerly listened to something Brian was saying.

"Can't you tell me who the suspect is?" Gloria begged.

Paul studied her face. "You know I would if I could but I can't." He tossed his plate in the can and closed the lid. "You'll know soon enough."

He nodded toward the house. "I'm dropping the cup off for testing on my way home so we can get all the results back by Monday."

Al Dickerson met them at the trashcan. "Everything was delicious. Thank you for inviting me."

Liz was right behind him. "Yes, you really outdid yourself, Gloria."

It wasn't all Gloria. She had plenty of help from her friends. That was what friends were for. It had seemed like a lot of work though. Why did it take hours to get everything ready and only minutes to eat?

Paul and Gloria wandered from table-to-table as they stopped to chat with each of the guests. They all thanked her for inviting them and complimented the food.

Gloria brought out cups of coffee and paper plates filled with Oreo dessert. After everyone finished their coffee and dessert, they started to leave.

Jennifer and Tony were the first to leave. Tony pointed at one of his teenage sons who was chasing Mally around the yard. "The natives are getting restless."

Liz left next. "I have the longest drive home." She hugged Gloria and Paul and started toward her car. Al walked her out.

They stood beside Liz's car and talked for several long minutes before Liz climbed in her car and drove off.

Al crossed the yard and approached Gloria. "You and Liz seemed to hit it off," she observed.

"Yeah. We're just about the same age." Al grinned like a love-struck teen. "We're having lunch together next week."

Gloria touched his arm. "Good for you. Just watch out for Liz. She can be a handful," she warned.

Al gazed in the direction of where her car just pulled out. "Yeah. That's what I like about her. She has some fire left."

That was an understatement. She hugged Al good-bye.

One-by-one, the rest of the Garden Girls departed. Gloria made to-go plates for each of them.

Andrea and Brian were the last to leave. "We can help you finish cleaning up," Andrea offered.

The foursome wiped the tables and stacked them against the garage wall. They folded the chairs and carried them to the barn.

While the two of them chitchatted with Paul, Gloria made two more to-go plates. She hugged Andrea and Brian. "Thank you so much for all your help today."

Andrea grinned. "My pleasure."

Gloria and Paul stood close together on the porch as they watched the last two guests leave. Brian walked Andrea to her car, opened the door and waited for her to climb in.

They spoke for several moments before he closed her door and headed to his SUV. He lifted a hand and waved before climbing inside and following Andrea onto the road.

"Two for two," Paul said.

Gloria whirled around. "Huh?"

"Two for two on your matchmaking."

They settled in on the porch for a cup of decaf coffee. Gloria's feet were sore and her back stiff.

It had been worth it. She was glad Paul was finally able to meet all of her friends. They were an important part of her life, just like Paul.

"Will you call me and let me know the fingerprint results?" she asked.

He nodded. "After we make an arrest."

Gloria's heart stopped. Someone she knew. Possibly someone that was at her own house that very evening – was a cold-blooded killer.

He eased out of the chair. "I better go. I have to stop at the station on my way home," he reminded her.

Paul headed to the bedroom to retrieve the cup while Gloria fixed one final to-go plate.

She grinned as she glanced at all the leftovers still in her fridge. Her friends made sure to leave plenty for her.

"Don't fret too much over this Gloria."
Paul was behind her now. "There's nothing you
can do about it." He took the plate from her hand
and set it on the table nearby before wrapping his
arms around her and pulling her close.

She closed her eyes, laid her head on his
chest and took a deep breath. He smelled so
nice. Like a mixture of musky leather and fresh
outdoors.

Sudden tears burned the back of her eyes.
Someone she knew, someone she was close to -
was about to have their world ripped to shreds.

She pulled her head back and gazed up,
looking for a smidgen of reassurance that
everything was going to be okay.

Paul touched the side of her face. "At least
it's not you."

Gloria let out a snort and sob, all rolled
into one. "That's good to know."

"Maybe you're right and I'm wrong and the killer is this Toscani fellow or even Judith. I've been known to be wrong before," he admitted.

True. Still, he seemed confident.

He grabbed the keys from his pocket before leaning forward and kissing Gloria softly. She followed him onto the porch.

With one last good-bye kiss, he was gone. She stood there and waited until his taillights were out of sight before heading back indoors.

Chapter Sixteen

The church parking lot was packed the next morning. Nice weather always filled the place. There were only a few empty sections open near the back of the church.

Gloria slid into an empty spot and set her purse down.

Slick Steve plopped down beside her. *I really need to get out of the habit of calling him that,* she thought.

"Thanks again for inviting me to your cookout. It was great." He sounded sincere. "Your sister, Liz. She's something else."

"Yes, she is," Gloria muttered. She didn't have a chance to add to it. Dot and Ray slipped in on the other side.

"Your party last night was just what we needed," Ray confided. "It was nice to take our minds off our troubles and enjoy good company."

Gloria swallowed the lump that lodged in her throat. At least the two of them had a final fun night out before they hauled Ray off to jail the next day.

She reminded herself she didn't know Ray was guilty. For all she knew, it was Brian Sellers.

What about Steve? She glanced at him out of the corner of her eye. *What if it was Steve?* Her eyes flew open. She had never considered him.

What possible motive could he have? Yes, he was an outrageous flirt and left a trail of broken hearts. Was he hot after Dot?

She shook her head. No, it wasn't Steve. She felt guilty that she almost wished it were...or better yet, Judith.

After the service, the girls met in their usual spot outside.

Gloria turned to Ruth. "Do we have any shut-ins today?"

Ruth shook her head. "No. Believe it or not, everyone seems to be out and about. Must be the nice weather," she said.

"How's the house shaping up?" Margaret asked Andrea.

Margaret didn't live far from Andrea's new place. She passed it every day on her way to town, taking note of the transformation.

"Another few weeks and I'll be ready for a housewarming party," Andrea told the girls. "Say, you want to come by and see the progress?"

The girls agreed today was a perfect day to check out the old Johnson mansion. "I'll bring leftovers for lunch," Gloria offered.

They all parted ways with a plan to meet up at Andrea's at noon.

Gloria pulled in Andrea's drive right on time. She was surprised at how much the construction crew had accomplished since her last visit.

The outside was finished. A fresh coat of yellow paint covered the boards and bright blue shutters greeted guests as they meandered up the drive. Andrea made the right choice in colors, Gloria decided.

The rotting front deck had been replaced with smooth, new boards and the wrought iron railing had been power washed and painted a shiny black. The majestic plantation-style home would fit in perfect in the South.

The girls wandered indoors to check the progress. Drop cloths covered every inch of floor in the dining and living room.

"I'm going for a more neutral gray in the living room with a deep red for the dining room," Andrea explained. "Red is good for digestion, at least that's what I read."

They followed Andrea to the kitchen. She led them over to the wall separating the kitchen from the small hall, directly across from the cozy, wood-paneled library. "I'm thinking of knocking this wall down and opening it up with a wide, granite bar area. What do you think?"

Dot nodded her approval.

"I think you should become an interior designer," Lucy said.

"I told her the exact same thing," Gloria said.

The group wandered onto the rear patio while Gloria headed to her car to grab the food.

The girls settled at the picnic table, passed the leftovers around and filled their plates.

Ruth was the first to bring up the subject of Andrea and Brian Sellers. "Brian Sellers seems to have taken a liking to you," she commented.

Andrea blushed. "You think so?"

Margaret agreed. "Oh yeah. He was giving you the googly-eyes." She lowered her eyelids and winked seductively for emphasis.

"He did ask me if I was free for lunch one day next week," Andrea admitted.

"And?" Lucy prompted.

Andrea nibbled on the end of her hot dog. "I gave him my number," she said.

The group discussed his merits...his past career as a judge, how ambitious and stable he appeared.

"And cute," Lucy pointed out.

Gloria wiped her mouth and laid the napkin on her empty plate. "He has a great sense of humor."

Lucy turned to her friend. "What made you decide to invite him? Did you just pop into his hardware store and say, "Come to my cookout Saturday night?"

"Kind of. I needed a propane tank for the grill." That part was true. Gloria didn't add that she stopped by the hardware store to interrogate him about the murder.

Dot knew...she knew Gloria all too well. "Gloria. You went there to question him about the murder."

"Well, I did ask him a few questions..." her voice trailed off.

Andrea set her half-eaten hot dog on her plate. "Why would he be a suspect?"

Dot explained how he had offered to buy the restaurant and how he wasn't giving up. "That doesn't make him a suspect, though."

The conversation reminded Gloria of the imminent arrest. She pounded her fist on the table. "We have to find the killer and fast."

The group jerked back in surprise. A burst of anger out of Gloria was a rare occurrence.

She told them how she turned Judith and Brian's prints in for testing to see if they matched the print they found on the toilet bowl cleaner.

She didn't mention that Paul kept a cup from the cookout the night before for testing.

She abruptly got up from the table. The whole thing upset her every time she thought about it. The clock was ticking and she had no clear suspect.

Lucy, distracted by a more pressing matter, frowned. "What – no dessert?"

"I swear, Lucy. I've never seen anyone with a sweet tooth like yours," Ruth said.

"When you die, we're going to have a chocolate fountain at your wake in your honor," Margaret teased.

Gloria was the last to leave the small get-together.

Andrea walked her to her car. "Do you think there's a chance Brian did it?"

Gloria slowly shook her head as she remembered Paul's words. "My gut says no." She sighed. "Tomorrow. We should hear something tomorrow."

Andrea could see Gloria was visibly upset. She wasn't sure why since Gloria barely knew Brian.

Andrea pushed her sunglasses on top of her head and rubbed her brow. "I just wish someone had caught a glimpse of the killer out behind the restaurant that day."

Gloria was halfway to her car when Andrea remembered something. She had seen someone that morning in the vicinity of the restaurant and she recognized the person from the party the night before.

She waved her hands frantically at Gloria to stop.

Andrea rushed to the driver's side window. "I do remember seeing someone else that morning. I didn't know who that person was until last night at your party."

She went on. "The only reason I remember is their truck almost ran me over as they drove like a demon out of you-know-what coming from the alley behind Dot's that morning."

Gloria's eyes widened, her heart thumped in her chest. She reached out and grabbed Andrea's arm. "Who was it?"

The color drained from her face when Andrea told her the name. Gloria thought she was going to faint.

It all made perfect sense...in a horrible way.

There was one person Gloria was certain could confirm her suspicions. "Promise me you won't tell anyone what you just told me," Gloria said.

Andrea nodded. "I promise."

Gloria's thoughts bounced back and forth like a ping-pong ball. The one thing lacking was motive.

Chapter Seventeen

Gloria pulled into Gus's garage, relieved to see the lights were on. She hurried from the car and walked to the front door. It was locked.

Gloria pressed her face against the overhead door window and peered inside.

She could make out the corner of Gus's head, buried deep under the hood of a car. She tapped lightly on the glass pane.

He poked his head around the corner and waved when he spotted her, and then motioned her to the front door.

Gus unlocked the door and opened it wide. "Hi Gloria. What's up? Annabelle giving you problems?" he asked.

She shook her head. "No, Gus. Annabelle is fine."

"I'm sorry to bother you. I'll make this quick." She paused. "Jennifer. Jennifer Barrett's car. She had it in here not long ago."

Gus nodded. "Yeah a couple times now." He tapped the wrench against the palm of his hand. "The first time for a tire blowout. Not long after the tire, she was having trouble with her brakes. They went out on her," he explained.

Gloria took a breath. She had another question, but Gus answered it without her even asking.

"Suspicious, too. I would almost bet money someone cut her brake lines."

"You think it was intentional?" she asked. "That they had been cut on purpose?"

He nodded. "Without a doubt." He made a cutting motion with his fingers. "A clean cut straight across."

"I appreciate your time, Gus. You've been very helpful. " She turned to go.

Gus started to shut the door and stopped. "The police were in here a couple days ago asking about the car, too. You don't think someone was trying to hurt Jennifer?"

"I hope not, Gus. I hope not."

When Gloria got home, she dialed Dot's number. Dot picked up right away and Gloria got right to the point. "The day of the poisoning - did Jennifer have her car or did Tony drop her off?"

"Oh gosh, Gloria. That day is such a blur. Let me think." There was a long pause on the other end of the line. "No. I think her car was in the shop that day. She had a tire blowout."

"So Tony dropped her off that morning?"

"Hmm. Yes. I believe he did," Dot answered.

Gloria's mind was spinning. *What if it was Tony? If it was Tony, what was the motive? Money? No, they certainly didn't have a lot of money, especially since Tony's hours at the shop had been cut.*

"Thanks, Dot. I gotta run." Before Dot could ask too many questions, Gloria hung up the phone.

Gloria paced the kitchen floor. *Where was the motive? Unless... unless there was a life insurance policy. How could she find out?*

Gloria couldn't find out, but she knew someone else who might.

She dialed Andrea's number. "Hi Gloria."

"Hi Andrea. I have a favor to ask."

"Sure. Anything."

"Since you own an insurance agency, is there any way to find out if someone recently took out a life insurance policy on – say – their spouse?"

Andrea paused. "There isn't a national database that I know of - but there are other ways to find out. I'll need full names and addresses. Their date of birth would be helpful, too."

Gloria wouldn't be able to get their birth dates without raising a red flag but she could easily figure out their address. "I'll call you back in five minutes."

She raced to her computer, typed in Anthony Barrett, Belhaven, Michigan. Tony and Jennifer's address popped up on the screen.

She jotted the address on a slip of paper before heading back to the phone. She thought about calling Dot, to ask for Jennifer's birth date but she didn't want to cause concern.

She called Andrea back and gave her the information.

"I'll call you back within the hour," Andrea promised.

Gloria hung up the phone and started to pace again. Maybe it wasn't about money. Maybe Tony was seeing someone and wanted to get Jennifer out of the way. Either way, the whole situation was tragic.

She was still pacing when the phone jarred her back to reality. "What did you find out?"

"What do you mean, 'What did you find out?'" It was Paul.

Her phone beeped. Another call was coming in. "I'll call you right back."

She disconnected and answered the second line. "Hello?"

"You were right. Someone took out a life insurance policy. A *large* life insurance policy on Jennifer Barrett – to the tune of eight hundred-fifty grand not more than two months ago."

"I need to tell Paul," Gloria blurted out.

"Let me know if I can help in any other way," Andrea replied before the line went dead.

Gloria's fingers trembled as she dialed Paul's number. "What was that all about?" He sounded annoyed.

"It was Jennifer's husband, Tony. He cut her brake line right after he slashed her tires. When that didn't work, he snuck in the back door of the restaurant and dropped poison in Dot's pot of dumplings, thinking that Jennifer would be the first to try them."

Gloria paced the kitchen floor. "The only problem was, by the time he grabbed the cleaner and made it into the kitchen, Jennifer had already tried a sample and was in the front waiting tables."

Paul confirmed her theory. "We're working on his warrant now. As soon as the lab confirms the fingerprints first thing tomorrow morning, we'll be on his doorstep."

Gloria wasn't sure if she was relieved it wasn't Ray or heartbroken that it was Tony. He seemed like such a nice young man. What a shame. Jennifer's life was about to crumble around her...

Gloria spent the rest of the evening in a state of distraction. She couldn't even focus on her favorite detective show.

She crawled into bed early but spent the night tossing and turning. Visions of Tony sneaking in Dot's place played out in her mind over and over like a b-rated movie.

Gloria gave up trying to sleep and eased out of bed just as the sun was coming up. She glanced in the bedroom mirror on the way to the kitchen.

Her hair was pointing straight out at various angles. It reminded her of a fashion model sporting one of those haircuts that everyone raves about being cutting-edge fashion.

She grinned at her reflection in spite of her somber mood. *I wonder what people would think if I left it like this all day,* she wondered.

Mally and Puddles met her in the kitchen. She fed them and then followed Mally onto the porch. Dark, ominous clouds filled the sky. Thunder rumbled in the distance. It was going to be a gloomy day...fitting for Gloria's mood and the events that were about to take place, and the lives that would soon be changed forever.

She started a pot of coffee and headed to the bathroom, pausing in front of the bathroom mirror as she studied her reflection again.

Gloria turned her head this way and that. She reached up and raked her bangs forward with her fingers before she fluffed the back up. She nodded in satisfaction and decided she would leave her hair just like that.

She turned the shower handle on high and the cool water brought her to life. It was amazing something so simple could improve her state-of-mind.

With the shower over and her brand new hair-do in place, she poured a cup of coffee and reached for the morning paper.

She had just finished her coffee and started to pour a second cup when a car pulled into her drive. It was Dot. She glanced at the kitchen clock. The breakfast crowd would be in full swing at the restaurant and she wondered why Dot wasn't at work.

Gloria waited at the door as Dot headed up the porch. From the look on her face, Gloria knew that police had arrested Tony.

She flung the door open and stepped to the side to let Dot in. "You'll never guess what," Dot said.

"They have a suspect in Mike Foley's murder," Gloria replied.

Dot set her purse on the kitchen table and plopped down in a chair. "How did you know?"

Gloria poured a cup of coffee for Dot and set it in front of her. "Paul told me he thought there would be an arrest this morning." She wasn't sure how much she should tell Dot she already knew.

"Did you know it was Tony?" Dot asked. "Is that why you called last night to ask if Tony dropped Jennifer off the morning of the poisoning?"

"Yeah. I didn't put the pieces together until last night," Gloria confessed. "It was right after I stopped by Gus's shop and he told me Jennifer's brake lines had been intentionally cut."

Gloria wasn't sure what else to say so she took a sip of coffee instead. "You want a donut?"

Without waiting for an answer, she pulled the box from the corner pantry and set it on the table. Chocolate made everything better.

She opened the lid and picked out a chocolate éclair before sliding the box across the table.

Dot plucked a glazed donut from the box and closed the lid. She absentmindedly broke off a chunk and chewed.

Gloria tore her éclair in two pieces and licked the creamy filling before continuing. "Andrea told me she saw Tony the morning of the killing, that he tore out of the alley behind the restaurant so fast he almost hit her."

"She just remembered that?" Dot asked.

"Well, she didn't know who Tony was until the cookout the other night and the sight of him jogged her memory."

Dot's eyebrows furrowed. "So he snuck in the back door of the restaurant and dumped the cleaner in my dumplings..."

"Yep. Thinking that his wife would be the first to try them like she always does."

Dot shook her head, as if to clear it. "Unbelievable." She squinted at the watch on her wrist. "I better get going. Ray is holding down the fort by himself."

Dot was out the door and across the porch before she stopped and turned back around. "By the way, I'm not sure what you did to your hair but I love it. It looks so..."

"Trendy?" Gloria suggested.

Dot slowly nodded. "Like something one of those fashion models in a magazine would wear."

Gloria grinned. "Thanks. I like to call it bed head."

"Ha," Dot snorted. "Well, whatever it is, it's working for you."

Gloria watched as Dot pulled out of the driveway and headed back into town.

She eased the porch door shut. There was still something she couldn't quite put her finger on. It was nagging at the back of her mind and it was just out of reach.

Gardening always cleared Gloria's head. She pulled on an old pair of work shorts and t-shirt before she slid her feet into her garden boots. "C'mon Mally."

Mally trotted over to the door and waited for Gloria to open it. They headed to the barn first where Gloria grabbed packets of radishes, cauliflower and carrot seeds from the wooden shelf on the back wall.

She pulled a metal trowel from a hook by the door on her way out.

Gloria had tilled the garden a few days earlier. She shoved the trowel in the rich soil and tossed the clump to the side. She dropped radish seeds in first, careful to sprinkle the seeds in a straight line. She covered them with a scoop of dirt and then finished her task with a gentle pat.

She started on a row of carrots next, following the same methodical system. Dig. Drop. Scoop. Pat.

Mally trotted over to investigate just as Gloria started on the cauliflower. She tromped right over the top of the freshly planted radishes.

Gloria stopped what she was doing and led her off to the side. "Sorry girl. The garden is off limits from now until fall, everything has been harvested."

She continued working on the cauliflower while Mally sat on the grass at the edge of the garden and stared at her. Her eyes begged to be allowed back in the garden.

Gloria eased off her aching knees and pushed herself to her feet. She tiptoed past the tidy rows as she made her way over to Mally. "Good girl. No more garden until fall," she reminded her.

The gardening cleared her head but it didn't help with the itty-bitty nudge that was ping ponging around. She was missing something...something important.

The house phone started to ring as she leaned over the kitchen sink and scrubbed the dirt from her hands. She grabbed the nearest towel and wiped them dry. "Hello?"

It was Paul. "We arrested Tony a couple hours ago."

"I heard." Gloria hung the towel on the stove handle. "Dot stopped by a little while ago."

They talked for several long minutes. She didn't mention the fog in her brain and the small something that was driving her crazy. In each of her investigations, there had been some little detail, some small clue right under her nose that she was staring straight at, yet couldn't put her finger on until the very last moment. Until it was almost too late.

Maybe there wasn't anything more this time. It just seemed so cut and dried. So open and shut. Perhaps, for once, she was making something out of nothing. At least that was what she tried to convince herself.

Her stomach grumbled and she glanced at the clock. A trip to Dot's restaurant for lunch was in order.

She changed out of her gardening clothes, tossed them in the laundry basket and checked her hair one more time. The more she looked at it, the more she liked it.

There was only one problem. How could she replicate what her pillow had created overnight?

Gloria grabbed her keys, headed toward the kitchen door and then paused. She had a stop to make to a special place she visited every couple of months. Her visit was long overdue.

Gloria reached inside the kitchen closet and pulled out a large plastic bag before heading to her car.

Dot's restaurant was packed. The only parking spot she could find was at the end of Main Street, right in front of the Nails and Knobs Hardware Store. She peeked in the front window and spotted Brian in the back of the store helping a customer.

Gloria opened the door and stepped inside. She wandered around the store as Brian finished helping his customer. After the man left, she made her way over to where he was standing behind the counter.

"The murder has been solved." Brian tipped his head to the side, his eyes twinkling. "I guess it wasn't me," he teased.

Gloria wasn't going to let him ruffle her feathers. "A good detective needs to follow up on every single lead."

"True." He leaned forward. "Were you able to figure out who it was?"

"Barely," she admitted. "It took me until late last night."

His expression grew grim. "Such a shame. They seemed like such a nice couple, too."

Gloria couldn't agree more and she felt guilty. Guilty that she was glad it wasn't Ray or Dot.

Gloria had a sudden thought. "I'm heading down to Dot's for lunch. Care to join me?" she asked.

The dark look left his eyes and the twinkle returned. "Aren't you afraid people will start talking? Dinner Saturday night and now lunch today?"

Gloria snorted. "Hey, if they think I can hook someone almost young enough to be my grandson, then I say gossip away."

He grabbed his jacket and keys from the hook behind him. "I think you're selling yourself short. You're one hot lady." He followed her out the front door and then locked it behind them. "You did something to your hair," he added. "I like it."

Gloria reached up and touched the stiff spikes. "You do? Really?"

He grinned as he took her arm and they began walking. "Yeah. It gives you that 'cougar' look."

Gloria grinned. "You missed your calling. I think you should've been a comedian."

She changed the subject as she glanced at him from the corner of her eye. "Andrea told me you invited her to lunch."

She had caught him off guard. "Yeah. We really hit it off the other night." He had a sudden thought. "Say. You weren't playing matchmaker..."

It was Gloria's turn to smirk. "Maybe."

"You did." He shook his head. "You're a jack of all trades. Super sleuth, matchmaker, and chef extraordinaire."

"Keep it coming," she joked.

They were in front of Dot's now. He opened the door and Gloria stepped inside. The place was packed and the noise level at an almost deafening pitch. Gloria would bet money the buzz was about Tony's arrest.

Heads turned as the odd couple made their way to an empty table in the back. Ray spied them right away. He set two water glasses and two menus on the table. Gloria didn't bother looking at the menu. She knew every item on it by heart.

"Coffee?" Ray asked.

Gloria shook her head. "I better stick with water."

Brian looked up from his open menu. "What is today's special?"

"Roasted chicken with two sides," Gloria answered.

"I'll have that," Brian decided.

"Make that two," Gloria added. "I'll have a salad and vegetable medley for my sides."

"Ditto," Brian said. "I'll make it easy on you."

Ray jotted down the order and then tapped his pen on the notepad. "That's a shame about Tony."

Gloria's expression grew grim. "I know. So hard to believe..." Her voice trailed off. A tinge of guilt washed over her when she remembered for a brief time, she suspected Ray. *What was she thinking?*

Gloria stared at Ray's back as he walked away. She turned to face Brian, who was studying her expression.

He nodded at Ray. "You thought it may have been Ray," he observed.

"How do you do that?" she asked.

He answered her question with one of his own. "What? Figure out what's going on in someone's head?" He leaned back in the chair and crossed his arms. "Remember, I was a judge. You become somewhat of an expert at figuring out what makes people tick."

Gloria grabbed her straw and swirled the ice in her glass. "I guess that makes sense."

His expression grew serious. "So you think Andrea and I are a good match?"

Gloria rested her chin on her fist as she studied his face. She mentally ticked off all the reasons she liked him. He was smart. He was funny. He was financially secure. He was single.

He was a good-looking guy. The more she knew, the more she liked.

Still, her number one concern was Andrea. Gloria was protective of her young friend. She couldn't bear the thought of her getting hurt.

Belhaven was a small town and eligible bachelors, especially ones like the one sitting across from her, were few and far between.

She answered as honestly as possible. "I think you two could be a very good match." Her eyebrows drew together for a second. What if she did a little investigative work on him, find out if he was on the up-and-up? For Andrea's sake, of course. "Only time will tell."

He didn't get a chance to answer. Ray was back with their lunch. The roasted chicken looked delicious. She sliced off a small piece to sample before digging into her salad.

The two chatted easily about life in a small town and his plans for the corner grocery and drug store. She popped a piece of lettuce in her mouth and chewed thoughtfully. "I never see you working in the grocery or drug store. Just the hardware store."

"I have to confess, the hardware store is my favorite. The smells, all the neat gadgets and tools." He shrugged his shoulders. "I have good people running the other two and the businesses don't need much of my time."

"You know Andrea owns an insurance agency in Green Springs."

Brian nodded, his mouth full of broccoli spears. "Mmhmm."

"She's fixing up the old mansion on the hill, not far from your place."

He swallowed his food. "She told me to stop by one day and she would give me the grand tour."

They were still chatting away when Lucy and Margaret stopped by on their way out the door. "You two better watch it. Tongues will start wagging," Margaret warned.

Gloria waved a hand in the air. "Oh stop it."

"Poor Paul," Lucy teased.

Margaret leaned forward, tapped Gloria's shoulder and whispered in a low voice. "Dot said you figured out it was Tony."

Gloria nodded. "Yeah, it took me awhile."

Lucy patted Gloria's shoulder. "Three for three."

Gloria had to admit she was getting good at sleuthing. Now if she could only figure out how to make a little money on the side, not that she needed it. She remembered the gold coins hiding in plain sight inside her kitchen. "I met with some attorneys the other day to talk about writing up a will." Gloria gave Margaret a meaningful stare.

Brian set his fork down. "You don't have a will?" He was surprised. Gloria seemed to have it all together. At her age, she should have a will. "I can recommend a good one, if you need."

Gloria had already decided on the woman she had met. *What was her name? Melissa, Clarissa?* "Do you know a Patricia Caldwell?"

Brian nodded. "She's good," he confirmed. "There's also Evan Tate."

Evan Tate was another one of the other attorneys Gloria had met with the other day. "I met with him, too."

"You can't go wrong with either one," he said.

"We can talk about it later." Margaret was using her "don't say too much" voice.

"Gotcha."

Ray returned to pick up the dirty plates and set the bill on the table. Gloria and Brian reached for it at the same time. Brian got to it first. "You can get it next time," he bargained.

She pulled her hand back. "It's a deal. But I invited you," she pointed out.

"True," he agreed. "Let me be a gentleman." He leaned forward and whispered conspiratorially. "What will everyone think if I can't even buy my girl lunch?"

Gloria rolled her eyes. "Okie doke. Lunch is on you."

Gloria nodded to a few of the diners as the two of them made their way back outside. Brian and she meandered along the sidewalk as they headed back to the hardware store, enjoying the tiny bit of sunshine peeking through the heavy rain clouds.

They stopped in front of Annabelle. "Thanks again for lunch."

He nodded. "We will have to do that again soon. It was nice to take a break."

He unlocked the hardware store, juggling the keys in his hands. "You know, I don't think I want to buy Dot's place anymore. Belhaven needs a place like that."

He rocked back on his heels and crossed his arms. "If you could think of one thing this town needs – other than a good restaurant, something you currently have to drive to the next big town to get, what would it be?"

Gloria's first thought was a bank. It was a real pain in the rear having to run all the way to Green Springs every time she needed to do her banking. To her, it was a no-brainer. "A bank."

As long as he was asking, she had something else to throw out there. "And maybe expand your grocery store. It's nice and everything, but bigger is better, especially for food. Plus, if you did, I can guarantee it would be worth your while."

"I'm one step ahead of you on that one," he said. "I already have an architect working on a set of prints for an expansion. I plan to double the size of what we currently have and add on a small bakery with a gourmet deli."

Gloria loved the idea of being able to drive into town and pick up deli treats. Plus, it would create more jobs for the small town, something they desperately needed. "I'll be your first and best customer," she promised.

A local resident met them on the sidewalk. He pointed to the hardware store. "You open?"

Brian nodded. "Yep." He waved at Gloria before the customer and he disappeared inside.

Gloria slid in the driver's seat and started the car. She pulled out of the parking spot and headed in the opposite direction of home.

Chapter Eighteen

Gloria reached the edge of town where the road curved sharply. The drive from town was picturesque. A small, green valley dipped out of sight beyond the guardrail. It was a peaceful place.

Gloria didn't travel the road often, except when she was coming here. She made a sharp left as she pulled onto a small, rutted drive and coasted to the back.

Gloria looked around. The grass needed to be mowed, she decided. Weeds were beginning to sprout up here and there.

She stopped Annabelle in her usual spot, shifted into park and shut off the car's engine. She grabbed the plastic bag from the passenger seat and opened the driver's side door.

Gloria glanced down at her purse, lying on the seat next to her. There was no need to take it with her or even to lock the car. There was no one around.

She made her way to the front of the car and stepped across the gravel drive.

Up ahead was the familiar oak tree. The tree hadn't been there long and had been planted only a couple years earlier...when Gloria first started coming here.

The tree was getting big now. The leaves were pushing out, searching for the warm spring sun. The branches sprawled forward, as if to shade the place Gloria was headed.

The tree would find little sun today since the skies were gray and overcast.

Gloria would need no shade, but soon enough it would be summer again and the leaves a welcome cover from the oppressive heat.

Gloria strode forward, her feet sure of their destination.

When she reached the spot, she kneeled on the ground and leaned forward as she pulled the tall grass from around the edge of the marble marker.

Her hands tenderly brushed away the leaves and debris from the name etched on the surface. *James Rutherford.*

She talked to him as if he were right there in front of her. "What a gloomy day. Did you order this?"

"Oh, I brought some flowers to spruce the place up." She pulled the flowers from the bag and stuck a cluster of red geraniums near the family headstone...the one with James's name. Her name was on the other side.

"They're your favorite. Red geraniums," she added. She arranged several more near the edge before placing an Easter lily next to his tombstone.

"That reminds me." She leaned back. "You would be so proud of me. I remembered that it's too early to plant the tomatoes, but I got some radishes, carrots and cauliflower in the ground this morning."

She changed the subject. "The kids are all doing great. Jill came by with the boys the other day. We went to the flea market." She slid her finger across his name as she talked. "You wouldn't believe how big Ryan and Tyler are getting."

A lump lodged in her throat. She sighed as a tear trickled down her cheek. This was always the worst part.

A sudden breeze picked up and the wind whistled through the branches overhead. "I'll give them a hug from you," she whispered.

Gloria glanced at the gathering storm clouds. A drop of rain splashed the top of her hand. "I better go. It looks like it's going to rain." She choked back a laugh. "I guess you're trying to get rid of me, huh?"

She shifted forward and eased her aching knees from the hard ground. She put two fingers to her lips and softly kissed them before touching her fingertips to his name. "I love you."

Without saying another word, Gloria grabbed the empty bag and turned to go. With one last longing glance, she shuffled over to Annabelle and slipped inside. She started the car and headed back down the bumpy path and out the cemetery gate.

Chapter Nineteen

Gloria drove straight home from the cemetery. The familiar pain stabbed her heart and after all these years, she knew how the rest of her day would go. A fog of melancholy ache would stay with her for hours.

She knew in her soul that James was in a better place, keeping a watchful eye over her. He reminded her in simple ways he was still with her, even if it was in spirit.

Gloria unlocked the porch door and let herself inside.

Mally hopped out of her bed and wandered over to greet her.

Gloria bent down and wrapped her arms around Mally's neck. The dog stayed still as Gloria buried her head in the soft fur. *Thank you, God, for this dog's love.* When she stood back up, Mally thumped her tail softly and let out a low whine as if to say, *I love you, too.*

Gloria fed Mally and Puddles before she walked over to the fridge. She mindlessly pulled the door open and peered inside, although she wasn't hungry so she closed the door.

Instead, she made her way to the cupboard, grabbed a glass, filled it with tap water and headed to the living room.

The remote was on the stand next to her favorite recliner. She eased into the chair, reached over and picked it up. The news was on but it was just background noise. She stared at the screen, her mind a million miles away.

The phone rang and Gloria stared at it for a long minute...long enough for the ringing to stop. Maybe tomorrow. Tomorrow she would be ready to join the world again but not tonight.

Puddles jumped up on the recliner and settled onto Gloria's lap. Mally was there, too. She stared straight at Gloria. Not blinking.

"I guess you want up here, too." She pulled the lever on the side of the chair and the footrest popped up. Mally hopped up and squeezed in on the other side.

It was this exact position that the three of them drifted off to sleep. Tomorrow would be a new day and it would arrive soon enough.

Chapter Twenty

Gloria sat upright in her recliner, her heart pounding. Mally and Puddles were right next to her, in the exact same spot as when they had fallen asleep.

A dream had woken her and Jennifer was in it. Gloria could see her plain as day. It was so real, she was certain that if she reached out, she could touch her.

Someone was chasing Jennifer through her house.

Gloria couldn't get a clear view of the shadowy figure.

Jennifer was screaming at the top of her lungs. "Help me! Somebody help me!" The terror in her voice pierced the still air.

It was at that precise moment Gloria remembered. She remembered the nagging something that had been stuck in the back of her mind. It was something Jennifer had told Gloria at the party the other night, how her father-in-law, Fred, had borrowed her car just before the brakes went out, and that the car's brakes had been fine before he took it.

Jennifer had laughed, saying it was just her luck.

Maybe it wasn't bad luck. What if Tony's dad was in on it, too? What if he had cut her brake lines? If so, would Fred try to finish the job now that Tony was behind bars?

Gloria had heard rumors around town that Fred's sawmill was having financial troubles, how the whole place was in foreclosure and they were months away from losing it all. The house. The land. The business. Tony and Jennifer's place.

Gloria struggled to get out of the chair as she glanced at the clock on the wall. It was still early. Only 8:30 p.m.

Should she warn Jennifer? Tell Jennifer her suspicions? Would Jennifer even believe her?

Gloria was torn. To warn or not to warn. She decided to err on the side of caution. Before she could change her mind, she grabbed her car keys and purse and headed to the door.

She decided that if the lights were still on at Jennifer's house, she would knock on the door.

If the lights were off, she would wait until morning. She hopped in the car and headed out of town. It was time to tell Paul her suspicions.

She dialed his cell number, all the while focusing her eyes on the dark, deserted country road. Her eyesight, especially when she had to drive at night, wasn't what it used to be.

Paul picked up on the first ring. "I tried to call you earlier."

"I fell asleep in the recliner." It was true. She had.

"Listen, I had a dream. I think Jennifer Barrett's life is in danger."

Paul listened as she told him about the conversation Jennifer and she had had the other night at the cookout. "I'm on my way over there now."

"I'm right behind you," he said. "Please wait until I get there."

"I'll wait until the last possible minute," she promised. That was as close to a promise as she could make.

The Barrett home was lit up like a Christmas tree. Even the front porch light was on. Of course, Jennifer and Tony had teenagers and teenagers were like shadow people who slept all day and stayed up all night...

There was an empty farm field directly across the street from the Barrett's mobile home.

Gloria backed Annabelle onto a rutted path leading into the field and switched off the headlights but left the car running. She could see shadows moving around inside. Ten minutes went by and so did the shadow people as they moved back and forth.

Paul should be here any minute, she thought.

A dark figure rounded the side of the front porch deck, crept up the deck steps and made its way to the door.

When the shadowy figure reached the front door, the porch light illuminated the figure, revealing their identity.

Gloria's eyes widened. It was Fred - Tony's dad. She watched as he lifted his hand and rang the doorbell. He stood there for several long moments before he pressed the button a second time.

Gloria's eyes darted down the dark road. *"Hurry, Paul. Hurry!"* she whispered.

The door finally opened. Gloria could see the outline of a female figure. It was Jennifer.

The screen door swung open and Fred stepped inside. Jennifer closed the door behind them.

Drops of sweat formed on Gloria's brow. She rubbed her forehead and stared at the road. *What was taking Paul so long?*

Chapter Twenty-One

Jennifer Barrett was having an unbelievable day. It all started when the police knocked on her front door bright and early that morning.

They had an arrest warrant for her husband, Tony. At least they had allowed him to throw on some clothes before they read him his rights and put him in handcuffs.

They did it right in front of her and the kids.

Jennifer followed one of the officers out onto the deck and closed the door so her kids wouldn't hear. "What is going on? Why are you arresting my husband?" A sob caught in her throat when she saw Tony's hands cuffed behind his back as two officers guided him to the squad car.

"Murder and attempted murder," one of the officers replied.

Tears sprang up in her eyes. She started to chew on her lower lip. "Wh-whose murder?"

"Michael Foley."

"And the attempted murder?" she whispered.

The officer stared at her sympathetically. He hated this part of his job. He reached out to touch her arm but let it fall to his side instead. "Yours."

A loud buzz filled Jennifer's ears. The feeling was all-too-familiar. It was the feeling she got moments before she fainted.

She grabbed the edge of the porch chair and felt her way to the seat before easing into it. "I-I just can't believe it."

She watched as the cruiser pulled out of the drive. Jennifer could see Tony's dark head in the back seat. He was staring straight ahead. *Surely there must be some mistake. Did they have evidence against him? They must have.*

"....wait for someone to be here with you." The officer was talking but Jennifer missed most of what he had said.

She shook her head, as if to clear the cobwebs. "I'm sorry. I didn't catch what you just said."

"I asked if you wanted me to wait here with you until family arrived," he said.

"No. No, I'll be fine." A trace of irony touched her lips. "There is no one here but me," she explained. "My family lives out-of-state."

Jennifer's oldest son, Chad, stepped out onto the deck. He placed a protective hand on his mother's shoulder. "She'll be okay."

The officer nodded. This was the other part of his job he hated...when children were involved. "You sure son?"

Chad straightened his back, his mouth set in a firm line. "Yes sir."

Jennifer reached up, clasped her son's hand and squeezed it tightly. "I appreciate your concern," she told the officer.

Jennifer and Chad watched the officer climb into his car and drive off. Neither spoke as they opened the front door, stepped inside and closed the door behind them.

The rest of the day was a teeter-totter of emotion for Jennifer. There were moments she refused to believe Tony was capable of murder...or worse yet, capable of killing her. His own wife.

There were others when the pieces began to fall in place, how Tony had dropped her off for work the morning the man had been poisoned. She remembered telling him in the truck how much she loved Wednesdays at the restaurant because it was "Dumpling Day."

Jennifer told him how she sampled them every week and that Dot didn't mind.

He teased her, told her that she must be the restaurant's official "taster."

That particular morning was a bit different from others. Dot was usually in the kitchen working on something, but not that morning.

There was no one in the kitchen when Jennifer entered through the back door. She had noticed the huge, stainless steel pot of chicken and dumplings sitting on the counter. The rich aroma of creamy goodness filled the room.

Not wanting to miss her chance to taste test, she grabbed a bowl and ladled a small portion out. The restaurant was busy so she ate fast.

Jennifer rinsed the bowl and slid it into the empty dishwasher before she grabbed her apron off the rack and headed to the dining room.

It must have been then that Tony slipped in the back door and dumped the chemical in the pot. He must have thought his wife would return to the kitchen for a sample.

The next person to eat the dumplings was the poor man, Mike Foley, and his wife.

Her heart pounded loudly as she remembered the tire blowout and then her car's brakes giving out, causing her recent accident.

The house was quiet all day. The kids hid out in their rooms. She tried to talk to each of them one-on-one but they were as shocked as she was. Nothing she could say would make things better or bring their father home.

Dinner was a solemn affair. It consisted of grilled cheese sandwiches and tomato soup. Jennifer tried to eat her sandwich. It tasted like cardboard and a chunk lodged in her throat.

She left the rest on the plate and ended up dumping it in the trash.

Jennifer herded the kids off to bed a little later than usual, not that she believed any of them would get much sleep that night.

She turned the lights off in the kitchen when she heard a knock on the front door. She pulled the front curtain to the side and craned her neck to see who it was. It was her father-in-law, Fred.

For a second, she thought about not answering it, but her heart went out to him, certain he was as shocked as she was.

She unlocked the door and peeked around the corner. "Hi Fred."

"Hi Jennifer. Can I come in?" he asked.

"Sure." She nodded and stepped to the side.

His face, drawn and haggard, said it all. He looked tired. She wondered if she looked that tired. Probably.

He stood just inside the doorway, as if not quite sure what to do. "Would you like to sit down?" she asked.

He ran a ragged hand through his stark white hair and then nodded before making his way over to the dining room table. "I can't believe it," he said.

He walked right past the table and over to the sliding glass door where he began to pace back and forth. "How could they arrest Tony? Did they have evidence?" He stopped in his tracks and stared at Jennifer.

She shook her head. "I don't know. They must have."

The more Fred paced, the more agitated he became. He started to swear.

Jennifer grew alarmed. His actions were so uncharacteristic it was unnerving her.

She glanced at his jacket, his hands shoved in the pockets. Not once did he take them out. Jennifer caught a glimpse of something in his pocket...something shiny. A shiver of sheer terror ran down her spine.

It was at that precise moment Jennifer remembered Fred had borrowed her car the day before the brakes went out. *What if Fred **and** Tony had conspired to kill her?*

She swallowed nervously. Her eyes darted to the front door. She could make a run for it, but what about her children?

If she escaped, would she be leaving her children in the house with a killer? Would a grandfather murder his own grandchildren?

Jennifer's armpits grew damp. She reached out and grabbed the dining room chair in a death grip. Her knuckles turned white – the same shade as her face. *Think! Think!* She needed help and she needed it fast.

Fred was rambling now. She wasn't even certain he remembered she was there. "Uh, the kids haven't eaten yet. I was going to order pizza."

He paused for a moment and stared at her blankly. "Huh."

She didn't wait for an answer as she grabbed the phone and dialed 911. She pressed the phone tight against her ear and took a step back praying Fred couldn't hear the voice on the other end.

"911. What is your emergency?"

Her throat tightened and Jennifer choked out the words. "Yes, uh. I'd like to order a pizza. Deluxe," she added.

"Ma'am. Do you know you dialed 911?"

"Yes. Yes, of course. Make it a large with everything."

"Is there someone with you and you're unable to talk?" the operator asked.

"Yes. A double cheese and we need it delivered as soon as possible please." Jennifer closed her eyes, praying the 911 operator would understand.

"I'm dispatching a unit now." She rattled off Jennifer's address. "Does this person have a gun?"

"I'm almost positive. It's the same order I placed last week." Jennifer spied Fred out of the corner of her eye. He was coming her way.

"Okay, thank you very much. Twenty minutes." She disconnected the line before Fred got to her.

"I think you and I should go for a ride. It'll help me calm down," he said.

Jennifer jerked her head up and down. "Just as soon as the pizza arrives we can leave."

That answer seemed to satisfy Fred, at least for the moment. He walked back to the slider, stared out into the darkness and began to mumble under his breath.

Jennifer didn't dare ask what he was saying. She closed her eyes and prayed. She prayed for God's protection for her and her children.

The hands on the clock seemed to stop. She stared at the clock, willing the hands to move faster. Ten minutes. Fifteen minutes.

Fred stopped pacing and turned to Jennifer. "We can't wait much longer," he decided.

Jennifer's mouth was parched. She had trouble forming her words. "J-just a few more minutes. They should be here any second."

The doorbell rang. Fred was still on the other side of the dining room table near the slider. "Pizza delivery," a male voice called through the crack.

Jennifer hurried to the front door. She didn't bother peeking through the curtains as she threw the door open and dove behind an overstuffed chair next to the living room window.

Things moved fast after that. Armed police officers raced in while Jennifer crawled out onto the deck, her eyes shut as she prayed her kids would stay in their rooms.

When she opened her eyes, Gloria Rutherford was standing over her, her arms open wide.

A small cry escaped Jennifer's lips. She pulled herself to her feet and collapsed in Gloria's arms. Wrenching sobs shook Jennifer's slender frame.

Gloria held her for a long time. Tears filled her own eyes. The poor girl's heart sounded as if someone was ripping it apart.

Jennifer's back was to the door when the officers led a handcuffed Fred Barrett onto the deck and down the steps to the patrol car.

Paul was the last to step out of the house. He made his way over to Gloria and Jennifer.

Jennifer pulled herself upright. Her eyes were red, her face covered with splotches from crying.

She wiped her tear-stained face with the back of her hand. "D-did he have a gun in his pocket?"

Paul nodded. "Yes. I'm afraid he did." He reached out and touched her arm. "Your quick thinking saved your life, and your children's' lives."

Gloria was curious. "How *did* the police know to show up so fast?" She knew Paul was on his way but as far as she knew, he only suspected Fred's involvement.

"Jennifer dialed 911 and pretended to order a pizza. The operator caught on that Jennifer was not ordering a pizza but calling for help."

Gloria was impressed. "What a great idea. What made you think of that?"

A watery smile covered Jennifer's face. "I read in the paper awhile back how a woman was trapped in her home with her ex-boyfriend. He was holding her hostage. She dialed 911 and pretended to order a pizza."

Paul turned to Gloria. "I have to head back to the station and fill out paperwork." He touched Jennifer's arm. "Will you be okay if I leave?"

Jennifer hiccupped and laughed at the same time. "Do you think anyone else is still out there that wants to kill me?"

He shook his head. "No. I think you're safe now." He gave Gloria a peck on the cheek, made his way down the deck steps and disappeared into the darkness.

Gloria led Jennifer inside. "I'll stay awhile 'til things settle down. I have to say, pizza does sound good," she admitted.

She remembered she had skipped dinner earlier and was now starving. Maybe if they ordered pizza, she could get Jennifer to eat a little, too.

The pizza arrived and the girls each ate a piece as they talked about everything under the sun – except Jennifer's husband and father-in-law.

When Gloria was certain Jennifer had calmed, she gathered her belongings and headed toward the door.

She told Jennifer not to hesitate to call if she needed anything...anything at all.

She said a small prayer for the young mother, certain there were some tough days ahead.

Chapter Twenty-Two

The investigation into Michael Foley's murder wrapped up quickly and things once again settled down in the small town of Belhaven.

The new gossip around town was Andrea and Brian. They were almost inseparable.

Gloria was happy for them. They seemed the perfect couple and Brian doted on Andrea.

Andrea was spoiling him, too. She was trying her hand at cooking and getting good at it. Gloria was proud of her.

Andrea had planted a small garden next to the tool shed out back. She discovered she had a green thumb, and even experimented with fruits and vegetables Gloria never had any luck keeping alive.

Gloria planted the rest of her summer garden. It was shaping up quite nicely.

The only thing stuck in Gloria's craw these days were the coins. Her cousin, David, had contacted her a couple weeks earlier. The government got wind of the coins and were now claiming the coins were government property.

David was fighting it every inch of the way. He kept the girls up-to-date weekly but the case was dragging on.

Paul was busier than ever at the police station. It seemed that instead of slowing down, he was working even more.

Gloria finished watering her thirsty plants. She turned the faucet off and hung the hose on the side of the house.

The evening air temperature was perfect. Not too hot and not too cold.

She wandered up the porch steps and started to head indoors when she changed her mind. Instead, she slid into the rocker.

Mally met her on the porch. She plopped down at Gloria's feet, her head fell on her paws and she closed her eyes.

The scent of lilacs filled the air. Gloria closed her eyes. The smell reminded her so much of her grandmother.

A slideshow of memories danced around in her head. Happy memories. A small smile played across her face.

God had blessed Gloria in so many ways. She opened her eyes and rose from the chair.

"C'mon, girl. Time to head inside."

She opened the door and the two of them slipped into the kitchen for another quiet evening at home on the farm.

The end.

If you enjoyed reading "Death by Dumplings," please take a moment to leave a review. It would be greatly appreciated. Thank you.

Books in This Series

Who Murdered Mr. Malone? Book 1
Grandkids Gone Wild: Book 2
Smoky Mountain Mystery: Book 3
Death by Dumplings: Book 4
Eye Spy: Book 5
Magnolia Mansion Mysteries: Book 6
Missing Milt: Book 7
Bully in the 'Burbs: Book 8
Fall Girl: Book 9
Home for the Holidays: Book 10
Sun, Sand, and Suspects: Book 11
Look Into My Ice: Book 12
Forget Me Knot: Book 13
Nightmare in Nantucket: Book 14
Greed with Envy: Book 15
Dying for Dollars: Book 16
Stranger Among Us: Book 17
Dash For Cash: Book 18
Arsonist and Lace: Book 19
Book 20: Coming Soon!
Garden Girls Box Set I – (Books 1-3)
Garden Girls Box Set II – (Books 4-6)
Garden Girls Box Set III – (Books 7-9)

Get Free eBooks and More

Sign up for my Free Cozy Mysteries Newsletter to get free and discounted ebooks, giveaways & soon-to-be-released books!

hopecallaghan.com/newsletter

Meet the Author

Hope loves to connect with her readers! Connect with her today!

Visit **hopecallaghan.com/newsletter** for special offers, free books, and soon-to-be-released books!

Email: hope@hopecallaghan.com

Facebook: facebook.com/authorhopecallaghan/

Hope Callaghan is an author who loves to write Christian books, especially Christian Mystery and Cozy Mystery books. She has written more than 50 mystery books (and counting) in five series.

In March 2017, Hope won a Mom's Choice Award for her book, "Key to Savannah," Book 1 in the Made in Savannah Cozy Mystery Series.

Born and raised in a small town in West Michigan, she now lives in Florida with her husband.

She is the proud mother of one daughter and a stepdaughter and stepson. When she's not doing the thing she loves best - writing books - she enjoys cooking, traveling and reading books.

Dot's Delicious Chicken and Dumplings Recipe

Ingredients
1 Large Whole Chicken (remember to remove the giblets before boiling)
7 Cups Self-Rising Flour
1 Stick Butter or Margarine, softened
3 Tablespoons Season-All Seasoned Salt
Salt to taste (optional. 2-3 teaspoons)
Pepper to taste (approx. 2 teaspoons)
Water (2-1/2 cups to mix with flour)

Directions
Boil chicken in large pot until done – 30 minutes or it almost falls off the bone. Add pepper and 2 Tbsp. Season-All salt while chicken is boiling (plus additional table salt, if desired).

Remove chicken from pot when done and set it aside to cool. Let it cool long enough to handle with your hands for deboning. (approx. 30 min.) Debone when cooled.

Slowly start boiling the broth.

While the chicken is cooling, mix the flour and 1 tbsp Season-All salt in large mixing bowl. Scoop a hole in the center of the flour/salt mixture. Add margarine.

Using your hands, squish it between your fingers and dig into the flour, adding a small amount of water at a time to blend.

Knead the mixture until you have a big ball of dough.

Making the Dumplings

Using the flour mixture, pinch off a piece the size of a silver dollar. Carefully drop in slow boiling pot. Continue pinching off and dropping them in the broth until bowl is empty.

NOTE: You will have to stir often to keep the dumplings from sticking to the bottom of the pot.

Add the deboned chicken to the pot of boiling broth and dumplings. (Chicken and broth should be at a slow boil.)

After the chicken has been added, let simmer 10 - 20 minutes.

Remove from heat. Let stand for approx. 10 minutes before serving.

Enjoy!

Made in the USA
Middletown, DE
09 May 2024